Gone to the
Movies

Windsor, CA
https://www.ethanhuntwriter.com/

Print ISBN: 978-1-09835-867-9
eBook ISBN: 978-1-09835-868-6

Printed in the United States of America.

First Edition

Gone to the
Movies

ETHAN HUNT

Blue

"How's it going, buddy?"

The old, light blue truck squeaks as it hums along the highway. The rattles and wind noise sneaking through the windows grab Dustin's attention for a few seconds while he waits for a response.

"I'm okay," says Damon.

Dustin looks at the boy. He looks at his worn-out jeans with a hole in the knee and remembers exactly how they ended up like that. Damon was playing in the backyard under their deck at home. When Dustin asked him what he was doing, all he would say is, "I'm mining for gold." Dustin thought this was hilarious. Clearly their trip to try out gold panning in the foothills had stuck with the little guy. By the time Damon came in for dinner, he had worn a tiny hole in the knee of the pants. His mom, Holly, complained that she had just bought him those pants, but it was okay since the hole wasn't noticeably big. Damon kneeled to remove his shoes, and when he bent his leg, the hole ripped open into a giant gash and his entire knee protruded through. Mom was clearly frustrated, but all three of them had laughed in the end.

It was one of the good days Dustin could remember. Days that seemed normal. Days that had become exceedingly rare over the past few months. The jeans became Damon's favorite. Dustin thinks about how funny it is that something so damaged could become so important to a person.

The truck hits a bump in the road, and a tiny laugh escapes Dustin as he snaps out of his deep thought.

"What, Dad?" asks Damon

"Oh nothing ... just thinking about how good this truck's been to me."

"Oh," Damon replies, pondering his dad's answer.

Dustin realizes that Damon can't possibly understand the bond a person has with a truck they've owned for seventeen years. Dustin bought it brand new in 1978 when he was twenty years old, and he's never wanted any other vehicle. Damon, ten years of age, has only lived with Dustin and his wife since he was three, so the truck is just another fun place to play for him. The memories etched into the fading paint of the truck had become part of Dustin's DNA though. He used it to move in with Holly when they married, they drove it to pick up Damon when they adopted him, and he's used it for so many home projects, he's lost track. Anyone who knows him knows his truck, too. Here he is, taking it on another life-changing journey he hadn't necessarily planned for.

"How much longer, Dad?"

"What ... 'til we get there? Maybe forty minutes," Dustin replies.

"Where are we even going?"

Dustin takes a deep breath and exhales.

"Well ... we're going to try living in a new town for a little while."

"But why's Mom staying at home? Shouldn't she go with us? You said this would be an adventure, so why isn't she going?"

Dustin silently looks out the window. He can tell Damon suspects something isn't right, but feels it is too soon for that conversation. As complex as it is, explaining how they ended up on this ride, without making Damon feel like the sky was going to fall, would be difficult. Dustin will have to think more about his approach.

"This is a boys-only adventure!" Dustin says, trying to lighten things up. "At least for now," he continues. "Besides, I need to work, and I know there are jobs for me up here."

"Yeah, I know," sighs Damon.

A thick canopy of bright green trees shades the road. Sunlight peeks through, projecting many small dots of light onto the asphalt. It isn't obvious along this stretch of road, but a series of destructive fires had swept through the area not so long ago. This is why there is so much extra work here for Dustin. As they approach the small town, the signs of the fire become more apparent. Many structures are well on their way to being rebuilt, but almost as many are still just muddy plots in the ground. Most of the debris from damaged structures has been hauled away, but, every so often, a chimney stands as the last remaining sign of love and life that had occupied those grounds. Black and gray chimneys and concrete steps act as tombstones dedicated to the memories that burned to ash in the fires.

Damon is a skinny twig of a boy. African American, but still young enough to be unaware of people's differences, let alone realize that those differences sometimes cause people to behave awkwardly around each other. To Damon, Dustin is Dad, simple as that. Dustin's thinning dark hair, slightly freckled complexion, and farmer's tan are things Damon notices, but they'd never caused him to question how important the man is to him. He knows they look different and that he is adopted, but he feels loved.

Along with the ripped jeans, Damon is wearing his favorite shirt. It is red with white stripes and is a little too big for him. He leans forward to push his tiny frame up from the worn-out leather truck seat to see out the window.

"Dad?" he says. "What the heck happened to all these houses?"

"Remember the fires we saw on the news last year?"

"Sort of," Damon responds.

"Well, those fires happened here," Dustin clarifies.

"But where do people live?"

"Well, a lot of people have to live somewhere else or with their families. Some of them had enough money to buy another house. Some people are working as quickly as they can to rebuild."

"Are you going to help them?" asks the boy.

"Yep," says Dustin.

Dustin senses a bit of pride from Damon that they are there to help so many people. The reality is that Holly needs a break from family life for a while. Adopting Damon was a difficult change for both her and Dustin. They love Damon and have always been happy with their choice to adopt, but many days in the past year felt incredibly tense. It sometimes feels like a bomb that could explode at any second. Dustin can't figure out why, but Holly is constantly on edge and sometimes has full-blown panic attacks. Dustin thinks about how difficult it is to describe to Damon what she is going through. To the untrained eye, it might look like she is a quitter, lazy, or a bad mom. The truth is, at least for now, that this break is the best thing for everyone.

"But where are we going to live?" asks Damon.

"Well, Aunt Sarah has a friend here named Dora. Dora has a special little house she said we can stay in for a while."

"Is she my aunt too?"

"Who, Dora?" Dustin responds.

"Yeah."

These types of questions are normal for Damon. Understanding family is a challenge when so many people have come in and out of your life at his age.

"No, buddy," says Dustin. "She's just a friend who's treating us like family. You know?"

"Okay," Damon quietly responds.

After driving through town, they find themselves in an area completely untouched by the fire. Dustin can see their destination up ahead. A dirt-and-gravel drive and a drab mailbox invite them off the main road. It is the type of road where, no matter how slowly the car is moving, dust fills the air. As soon as Dustin turns into the short drive-way, he can see the house peeking from the trees at the end. Obviously very old, it is a yellow and white farmhouse that has been cared for well but is certainly showing signs of ageing. Big farming tools and tractor attachments are scattered around the lawn that surrounds the turning circle at the end of the driveway. Their rusty color and the extra grass growing around them indicate a lack of use in recent years. The way they are arranged, however, tells arriving guests just how much joy they still bring to the property and its owner.

Damon looks around and thinks, *This looks like a fun place, but it isn't home.*

Dustin, always logistically minded, double checks the handwritten directions on the scrap of paper he had set in the cup holder next to his seat.

Well, this is definitely the place, he thinks.

Dustin has had butterflies in his stomach for months. Today is no different. He does what he always does to persevere in the moment and takes a deep breath.

I guess this is where we'll be figuring things out, he thinks.

"All right man," Dustin exhales as he pushes the creaky truck door open. "Let's see what's goin' on."

Borrowed

Dora steps through the front door of the house before Dustin closes his truck door. It is clear to Dustin that she always knows when someone is approaching her house.

I bet she can tell the difference between every car that crunches along that gravel driveway, He thinks.

She had been expecting them, so there is no look of surprise or concern on her face as she stands atop the wide set of six painted stairs. The porch is covered, exactly the type of porch you would expect to find on an early twentieth-century farmhouse. The comfort and confidence she feels when standing on that porch radiate from her. She feels protected here. Her connection to the love and memories embedded in the battered wicker and wood furniture to her right is a tether to the past that she hasn't quite moved on from. On her left is, of course, a porch swing. Dustin quickly has a vision of Damon sitting there. All children like porch swings, and maybe Damon will find comfort on this one. Dora is dressed as though she is part farmer, part hippie. Her pants are a faded tan color, loose, and well-worn with stains. On top, two t-shirts, each a different earth-tone. The green outer shirt has a hole in it: no doubt the reason for the red, clay-colored inner shirt. Her hair is gray with some black left in it, and very curly. It sits just above her shoulders and the lack of tidiness indicates how practical a woman she is.

Dustin closes the truck door, and she says, "You must be Dustin."

"Hi. Yes, yes I am," he awkwardly replies.

Damon sits in the truck as if he knows the gravity of the situation. As if he knows he and his dad will start over in this place. Of course, he doesn't know that, but his instincts serve him well. He slowly reaches for the door handle.

"Come on buddy, let's go," Dustin quietly says to him through the open truck window.

The door on the truck creaks as it opens, and then creaks as Damon pushes it shut.

"Well, how was your drive?" asks Dora from atop the steps.

"Pretty uneventful," Dustin says as he smiles.

The smile was for politeness, not because he was actually happy about anything in particular.

"Good. And who do we have here?" she asks, looking at Damon.

"This is Damon. Dame, say hello," Dustin says as he nudges the boy in the back.

"Hi," Damon says quietly.

"Hi, Damon. Do you like lemonade?"

"Yes," he replies quietly.

"Well come on up here and get yourself some," she says as she waves an old towel at him. "Be careful on these stairs."

"Thank you so much for letting us stay here," says Dustin as he and Damon approach the porch.

"Well, it was good timing with my renters leaving town. And it's not much of a place, so don't get too excited," she says with a smirk. "Should we go check it out? You guys can come back and get your stuff after you see it," she says as if there was any chance the two of them weren't going to stay there.

Dora comes down the stairs and they walk around the right side of the house. The tiny building they'll now call home quickly becomes visible. It backs up tightly against the forest, and has a very narrow, covered stoop in front, only one step up from the ground. Dustin can see one window in the front, but ragged curtains prevent him from having a clear view of the inside. The place is so small that the window and front door dominate the front of the building.

Dora steps onto the stoop and opens the door. It isn't locked.

I bet nobody around here locks their doors, Dustin thinks. *Probably not much of value in here anyway.*

He walks past Dora into the tiny house and quickly sees everything it has to offer. Along the left wall is a set of kitchen cabinets with a sink and a two-burner electric cook top. There's no oven and no microwave.

Jeeez, is there even hot water? Dustin wonders.

To the right is a cushioned bench under the front-facing window. On the far-right wall is a cozy-looking chair with a small round table next to it. A few books are stacked on the table.

This'll be a perfect place to sip some coffee while reading the paper, Dustin thinks.

A twin bed fills the rest of the space in the room. This seems like an obvious place for Damon to sleep. Past the foot of the twin bed is a doorway leading to the smallest bedroom Dustin had ever seen. It has another twin bed, a small dresser, and an armoire for hanging up a few bits of clothing.

Dora finally steps into the building and asks, "Well, what do you think?"

"This is great," responds Dustin. "This is all we need."

Dora smirks skeptically at Dustin's politeness. Dustin, however, truly feels that this is all they need for now. Perhaps the simplicity of the situation will allow Dustin the focus he needs to help Damon thrive without his mom there.

Damon sips his lemonade and then asks, "This is my bed?" almost rhetorically.

"You bet buddy," Dustin responds.

"Okay," says Dora. "You guys can get your stuff and move it in if you want. Didn't look like you had much in that truck."

"Nah. Just clothes, sleeping gear, and my tools. And Damon's bike, of course," Dustin says as he smiles toward Damon.

"Well, okay," Dora says with a tone of finality in her voice. "You know," she continues, "they're showing a movie at the old drive-in tonight. I think it's the one with the talking toys in it."

"I noticed that place between downtown and here," Dustin says.

"Yep. You could walk from here, but I guess you'll be wantin' to back your truck in there with some sleeping bags or something."

"You read my mind," Dustin says with a smile. "What do you think, buddy?"

"Sounds good," Damon says with a brevity that he only uses when strangers are around.

"Alright. Let's go get our stuff. Thanks again, Dora."

"You're welcome," she says with a subdued smile.

Old

Dustin clutches two boxes of popcorn, one in each hand. He didn't buy any drinks because there are a few left in the ice chest he packed for the trip. He doesn't mind saving a few bucks too.

As he walks back to the truck where Damon waits, he notices that the entire place is run-down. The asphalt pavement is completely worn out, potholes scattered everywhere. The white painted lines between each parking spot are chipped and dirty, some no longer visible. Each row of parking spaces has a small hump so that when a car is parked, its hood is tilted up. This gives people sitting in the cars a clear view of the screen. Since they're here in a truck, they had backed into the space instead, tilting the truck bed up toward the screen. The truck bed is a perfect place to lean back and watch a movie under the stars. This drive-in still has the wired speakers that can be removed from a pole and mounted on a vehicle window. Setting one of these on the truck bed rail works fine for them. It certainly seems like the town enjoys coming to this antique landmark. Surely some are celebrating silently that this part of town didn't burn. Others there are hardly watching the movie at all but enjoying each other's company.

God. It seems like everybody knows everybody else. Classic small town, Dustin thinks.

"Hey man. Come grab these," Dustin says as he lifts the popcorn boxes over the truck bed rail for Damon.

He hops onto the tailgate and says, "The movie didn't start yet, did it?"

"Nope," Damon quickly responds, his eyes fixated on the commercials on the screen.

Dustin slowly eats a single piece of popped corn and looks up at the sky. It is a clear night, and he can see an incredible number of stars. It is just cold enough that Damon might need to climb inside the sleeping bag they had brought along. Dustin's mind wanders to another time they were out under the stars together as a family. Years ago, on the day before Independence Day, they were in a neighboring town to watch a fireworks display. Damon was four at the time, and Dustin was filled with excitement. He'd always loved fireworks when he was a kid, and this was one of the things he most looked forward to as a father. Every year, he would get to hold his little guy close while the fireworks startled them both. The shockwave from exploding fireworks would hit them both in the chest at the same time, causing them to hug each other even more tightly. He would do that until Damon didn't want to be held anymore. That was the plan. He knows now, sitting in the truck at the theater, that Damon is too old for that. This makes him feel sad, but he's also proud of the boy Damon has become.

He remembers more than the fireworks from that night though. He remembers the difficulty Holly experienced when around so many people in a crowded area. It was difficult for Dustin to enjoy the events if he thought his wife wasn't. There was one problem after another. Somebody sat too close to them, then somebody was talking too loudly, then some children were playing too closely. By that point in the marriage, Dustin spent much of his conscious thought scanning for these threats even though he felt like they were normal occurrences when around other people. They were to be expected, he always figured, but Holly never seemed to accept this. Instead of feeling free in a wide-open space with stars above and soft green grass below her feet, she felt trapped. She felt imprisoned and tortured by every minor transgression committed by the people around her. Dustin struggled in these moments. Every complaint and every exasperated sigh stole his attention away from the moment, away from the stars, away from the green grass, away from the fireworks, and, worst of all, away from their son. He still somehow managed to hold the boy tight and enjoy the fireworks, but he felt battle weary when the night finally ended. He didn't recognize it at the time, but each one of these experiences caused a tiny bit of resentment. Each incident by itself was manageable, but when added together over time he began to feel robbed. Robbed of his plan for his life with his wife and son.

Dustin quickly snaps himself out of the memory and resolves to enjoy this moment with his son. Dwelling on the past would not allow them to make sense of everything while in this new place. Dustin looks at Damon again. The little boy is at peace and seems content eating his popcorn and watching the movie, the light and color from the movie screen reflecting off his face and eyes. Dustin feels content too, but not happy.

There is still quite a bit of commotion from people entering the drive-in. It's obvious that people don't mind being late, as the movie is about to begin. Over the sound of car engines, tires scraping across pebbles from the worn-out asphalt, and people saying hello to each other, Dustin hears an extra ruckus not far from their truck. Initially, it sounds like local teenagers goofing around, but then Dustin hears one exclaim, "Ha ha ha, I hit it!" He quickly pushes himself up from his sleeping bag to look over the bed rail in that direction. He can see four or five teenagers, a few on the ground, and a few in the back of a truck bed, and they are throwing rocks at something. Dustin quickly fears the worst, but hopes they are aiming at one of the busted speakers on a pole. He lifts himself onto his knees to look further and his worst fear is realized. The boys are throwing the rocks at an animal. Dustin refocuses his eyes in the darkness and then a bright scene on the theater screen offers some extra light. It quickly becomes obvious that the animal is a dog.

Whose dog is that? Dustin thinks.

Damon finally sits up and says, "What's wrong, Dad?"

Dustin keeps his eyes focused on the incident and angrily shoots back, "Some kids acting like idiots."

"What are they doing?" Damon inquires further.

"I think they're throwing rocks at that dog," Dustin says as he pulls himself up by the bed rail.

He quickly glances around and doesn't see anyone else leaning toward intervention. He is new to this town, but he has no intention of standing by while these kids harass this dog.

Just as Dustin's feet hit the ground, one of the rocks hits the dog hard enough to startle it. The animal finally realizes it's in danger and darts away from the food scraps it was trying to eat. It is a medium-sized dog, and it has a black and white mixed coat like a border collie.

Did someone bring their sheepdog to the movies? Dustin wonders.

Upon further examination, its fur is dirty and matted, confirming for Dustin its homelessness. As Dustin approaches, the dog is becoming more frightened and begins moving more quickly. The danger of the rocks subsides, but is replaced with the greater danger of cars driving through the dark lot looking for a parking space. The dog takes a quick left turn, and a car slams on its brakes, narrowly missing it. This spooks the dog, and it runs to the right, toward the kids who started the incident. They are now barking at the dog and laughing. One of them grabs a small rock to throw.

Dustin grabs the boy's arm, pushes him against their truck, and yells, "Don't you throw another rock!"

The rest of the group quickly realizes the error of their ways, but it is too late to affect how frightened the dog is. It continues to run through the rows of parked cars toward the enormous movie screen. The dog is fast and looking for an escape route. It darts through a row of parked cars and, just as it leaps out into the next traffic lane, a car slams on its brakes just a little too late. The car hits the dog and violently shoves it four or five feet. The dog screeches out in pain. By this time, most of the drive-in guests have realized what is happening and begin paying attention. A few are approaching to see if they can help. The dog is terrified, limping in pain, and wandering in circles. Dustin watches the dog closely as he runs toward it.

Oh god, I hope his head isn't injured, he thinks.

Dustin and the owner of the car are the first ones to reach the dog. He is sure the dog will try to bite him if he gets too close. He very cautiously begins to move toward the dog. By now, the dog has given up on escape and has laid down to check its wounds. It's panting vigorously, letting out small whimpers every few seconds.

Damon finally catches up to his dad and Dustin yells at him, "Stay back, Damon! Go to the truck and bring me my sleeping bag, okay? Hurry!"

More people begin encircling the dog, but nobody inserts themselves between it and Dustin.

Damon quickly returns with the sleeping bag and hands it over to Dustin.

"Here, Dad."

"Thanks buddy," Dustin replies.

"Is it going to be okay Dad?"

"I think so, but we've got to get it to a doctor."

Dustin creeps forward with the sleeping bag, hoping it will protect him from the dog if it snaps.

If I can wrap enough of the bag around the dog from behind, maybe I can pick it up without it biting me, he thinks.

The dog looks at Damon, whimpers some more, and puts its head down, as if to surrender its entire being to the people around it. Dustin approaches from behind and begins to place the bag and his arms around the dog's mid-section. The dog lets him do this, but as soon as Dustin tries to pick it up, it snaps at him. Dustin was expecting this. It was clear it had rib cage damage, but Dustin knows he needs to get this dog loaded into his truck to find help. He waits a few moments to let the dog calm down, and then carefully tries again. This time it works. The shock and pain of the situation have clearly taken a lot out of the animal. It has given up on escaping and allows Dustin to gingerly carry it to his truck.

A middle-aged woman with curly reddish-blonde hair is following Dustin as he carries the dog. It is the owner of the vehicle who hit the dog, and she keeps repeating, "I am so sorry. I didn't see your dog!"

Dustin finally snaps, "It's not my dog! I'm just taking it to find some help. It's okay. You couldn't see it. Those stupid kids are responsible for this. If you want to help, go find their parents and tell them what happened!"

With a puzzled look on her face, she replies, "Well, there's only one animal doctor in town. Everyone who has an animal has her number for emergencies. Why don't I go to the front to call her and tell her you need help?"

As Dustin closes the tailgate on his truck, he lets out a deep breath to calm down. "That would be great. Thank you."

"Okay. My son and his girlfriend will tell you how to get there. James! Get over here and tell this man how to get to the animal doctor!"

New

Dustin had only driven through town one time, but knows the exact building James and his girlfriend described in their directions. Much of the downtown core is a mix of Victorian and Edwardian architecture. As it happens in towns like this, many of the former homes had been converted to businesses. Occasionally mixed in with the ornate architecture are simpler old-west-style buildings. These had primarily been erected in the early days of logging in the area. Fortunately, a local historical society keeps the buildings and icons of the past from eroding away into history. Old mailboxes, phone booths, and even hitching posts from a time when people roamed the streets on horseback are kept in pristine condition. Again, as is the case in many small towns, there is a stretch of buildings from the mid-twentieth century. These buildings are painted cinder block, with glass storefront windows and doors, and flat roofs.

It isn't a long drive from the theater to downtown; the entire length of town can be driven in less than five minutes. Dustin drives to the "white painted cinder block buildings" that James had described. Right in the middle of this stretch of newer buildings is the veterinary clinic. Then he sees exactly what James told him to look out for. The large window on the left of the storefront has a mural of animals painted on it. It's an incredibly colorful picture with rolling green hills in the background, a bright yellow and orange sun in the sky, and every conceivable farm animal and pet crammed into a wide landscape that filled the window from left to right. Sunny Day Veterinary Clinic is hand painted across the top of the mural.

Dustin swerves across the two-way road and parks in front of the clinic with his truck heading in the wrong direction. It's late enough that nobody is parked there, and there is no oncoming traffic to worry about. He jumps out of the truck and flings the driver's side door closed.

"I hope she called the vet!"

Damon replies, "Is the dog gonna die Dad?"

"I don't think so buddy, but we won't know how badly it's hurt until the doctor gets here. Where is she ..." he says as he glances through the windows.

Dustin knocks on the window even though he can clearly see there are no lights on.

Maybe we should go around back, he thinks as he looks again through his hands cupped against the window.

Just then, a light in the back of the clinic turns on. He quickly realizes the vet had come in through the back of the building. Dustin sees the silhouette of a person quickly making their way to the storefront. He can see long hair and is quickly reminded that the doctor is a woman. Cautiously happy that someone is there to help, he heads to the glass door inset from the storefront windows by roughly six feet. The walkway in front of the door is sloped up toward the doorway and covered in aqua-colored penny tile, many of which are cracked or chipped. The glass door has a metal handle on the outside, and a metal bar on the inside. The vet begins unlocking the glass door while Dustin waits impatiently. He is so close to the door that when she finally pushes it open, he must awkwardly back out of the way.

Before she says anything, he quickly says, "The dog is out here in my truck!"

The doctor is dressed in casual clothes, obviously interrupted while relaxing at home. There is nothing overly doctorly about her, but Dustin can see she has arrived at the clinic with a singular focus, to help this animal however she can. Her long dark hair floats in the air behind her as she quickly jogs past Dustin toward the truck. He catches up with her, jumps from the curb down into the street, and grabs the handle of the truck's tailgate. It squeaks as he opens it. He jumps up into the truck bed and is impressed when the doctor follows suit.

"Barb said she hit the dog with her car. How did you get her into the truck?"

"I wrapped her in the sleeping bag to keep her from biting me and then carried her," Dustin replies in a hurry.

"Okay," the doctor says as she thinks deeply about what to do next.

By this point, Damon had exited the truck and is watching from the curbside.

"Is it gonna be okay?" he asks the doctor.

"I think so. But we've got to get her inside to see if she has any broken bones."

Damon suddenly has a frightened look on his face as if he hadn't yet considered that the dog might have a broken bone or two.

"You guys stay here, I'll be right back," the doctor says as she leaps down from the truck bed onto the sidewalk.

She darts into the clinic and heads directly into the back. A few more lights flick on inside while Dustin and Damon wait outside. The dog lets out a tired, agonized whimper.

"Dad..."

Before Damon can finish, Dustin says, "It's okay buddy, she'll be fine."

He isn't sure of this, but it seems like the best thing to say to his son at the moment.

"No, Dad. I was going to ask how the doctor knows it's a girl."

Dustin thinks deeply on the question for a second. He has no idea how she knew.

"Well, cause she's a doctor, I guess," he finally says to Damon.

Just after he responds, the doctor reappears from the clinic with a small stretcher in one hand and a large syringe in the other. She had also put on a lab coat and hung a stethoscope around her neck. The coat and her wild dark hair float in the air as she quickly leaps back into the truck bed. As if she is a magician, a hair band suddenly appears in her hand, and she uses it to tie up her curly mane.

After a deep breath, she says, "I am going to give her something to settle her down, and then we'll move her to this stretcher. We need to have her on something more stable to carry her inside."

"Why?" asks Damon.

"Buddy…" Dustin interjects.

"No, it's okay," the doctor says in a soothing tone. "If she has a broken bone, we don't want it to move, honey. It might hurt a lot, plus we want it to heal nicely."

As she speaks, she squats down next to the dog in the truck bed. She removes a semi-transparent plastic cover from the needle end of the syringe. The dog, exhausted at this point, allows the doctor to gently touch her head.

"Hold her head down right here," the doctor says to Dustin.

Standing outside the truck in the gutter, he reaches over the truck bed rail and follows her instructions. She then grabs as much skin as she can behind the dog's head, bunches it in her hand, and pulls it away from the dog. She is then able to inject the sedative into the dog without it feeling much of anything.

"Let's let that take effect," says the doctor as she stands up in the truck bed and begins shuffling toward the tailgate to step down.

Dustin moves from the side of the truck around to the tailgate and awkwardly stands by in case the doctor needs a hand stepping down. She is clearly capable of getting down on her own and doesn't notice Dustin's attempt at chivalry.

"I'm Dustin, by the way," he says as he extends his hand for a handshake.

"Oh, right," she begins as she pulls a latex rubber glove off her hand and proceeds to reach toward Dustin's hand. "I'm Melissa. Doctor Melissa. Howard," she says. Then, visibly flustered by her broken sentences, she finally spits out, "I'm Doctor Howard," with a half-smile.

"Nice to meet you," Dustin responds as they complete a handshake. "This is my son, Damon," he continues as he turns to his left and opens his left arm to gesture toward Damon who is still standing on the curb by the side of the truck.

"Hi Damon," Melissa says while reaching her hand past Dustin to shake Damon's hand. Damon grasps her hand and shakes it the way his dad taught him to.

"Oh, that's a good firm handshake you got there Damon," Melissa says as she squints her eyes trying make a tough-guy face. Damon doesn't give much of a reaction and gently puts his hand back down by his side.

"Are you a real animal doctor?" Damon says as he looks back up at her.

"Damon, of course she's a real…," Dustin begins.

"It's okay," Melissa interjects. "Yes, I am a real animal doctor, Damon. Would you like to see some of my cool animal doctor stuff?"

Damon excitedly nods his head with his eyes open wide.

"Okay, how about you help your dad and me take this baby dog inside so we can fix her up?"

"Okay," Damon responds with nervous excitement.

Melissa smiles at Damon and positions herself to climb back into the truck bed. Once in there, she takes the stethoscope from around her neck and places the earpieces into her ears. She holds it against the dog and listens in silence for a few seconds.

"Okay, I think she'll be okay," she says to Dustin with a look of concentrated confidence. "Her breathing is pretty stable. No sign of fluid in the lungs. Will you come up here and help me load her onto the stretcher?"

"Sure," Dustin eagerly says as he begins jumping into the truck bed.

"What do you want me to do?" Damon says as he walks closer to the truck.

"Damon, when your dad and I are ready, we'll need you to hold the door to the clinic open. Can you do that?"

"Yeah," he responds as he quickly moves toward the glass door.

She then tells Dustin, "I am going to put the stretcher as close as I can, and we should be able to move her without her feeling much. You ready?"

"Yep," replies Dustin.

Melissa positions herself toward the front of the truck bed where the dog's hind quarters lay. Dustin squats down by the head. They both slide their arms underneath the dog. The dog wakes up a little, aware that something is about to happen, but the sedative continues to do its job of keeping her docile.

Melissa says, "One, two, three," and they lift the dog and gently set her on the stretcher. Dustin then slides off the truck bed and is again standing on the street. He leans over the tailgate to reach out and grab the stretcher. Melissa repeats, "One, two, three," and they gently slide the stretcher toward the tailgate. Melissa rotates the stretcher so she can step down to the ground. Once satisfied with the position of the stretcher and the dog, she places her right hand on the remaining open spot of the tailgate and jumps down to the street.

"You ready?" she says to Dustin.

"Yeah," he quickly responds.

She then asks Damon if he is ready. "You ready, Damon?"

Damon quickly opens the door and loudly says, "Yeah!"

"Okay, one, two, three." They use the handles of the stretcher to lift it off the tailgate. Dustin begins walking backward toward the clinic while Melissa tells him to watch out for the curb and the ascending walkway that leads to the front door.

"You could have faced the other way you know," she says with a smirk, ribbing Dustin a little for not thinking of this.

Dustin immediately envisions the various movies and television shows in which he's seen people carry a stretcher and realizes the error of his ways.

"Oh. Duh," he says as they begin walking through the door to the clinic.

As they enter the clinic, the first thing Dustin notices is how clean it is. In an instant, he understands how important this place is to Melissa. A center aisle leads to some counters in the back of the clinic. On either side of the aisle are rows of shelves with pet supplies on them. To the right, various types of dog and cat food are stacked on the shelves. To the left, various pet toys, feeding bowls, leashes, and such are meticulously organized on shelves and hanging on pegboards. On the walls are reminder posters to have pets vaccinated, spayed, and neutered and to bring in farm animals for various services. Dustin senses that it's as important to Melissa that animals are cared for as it is to their owners. At the back of the clinic are two counters. On the right is a counter for pets to be examined. On the left is a counter with a cash register for collecting payment. This counter also has enough room to take a quick look at a small pet. They carefully walk in between the two counters, through some saloon-style doors that only partially block people from seeing what is in the back. Dustin's back guides the doors open and the stretcher slides through the doors without disturbing the dog. Melissa then follows through the doors. In this back area she has much more room to work. There is a large area with a scale for big animals and a place to tie them up for examination. She had a couple washing basins, one in a sink on the right wall, and one on the floor in the area to the left. Dustin finally realizes that the right side of the room is for traditional pets, and the left side is for larger animals.

"Let's put her on that table," Melissa says, gesturing toward a stainless-steel table in the middle of the floor on the right side. It is large enough to set the stretcher on while still leaving room to move the dog onto it. Dustin turns his head to his left to see the table, then begins guiding the stretcher over to it by walking backward and sideways. They lift the stretcher up a little, and then set it down gently on the table.

Taking a deep breath, Melissa then says, "Okay. We're not going to leave her on this table. We're going to wheel this table over to the x-ray machine, and then move her onto it."

"Okay," Dustin quickly responds.

Melissa uses her foot to release the brakes on the wheels closest to her. Dustin twists his head downward to look for the switches on his side.

"You got it?" she asks.

"Ah, there we go," Dustin responds as he releases the first brake.

He releases the second one very quickly. They gently guide the table across the floor to the x-ray machine. It is against the same wall as the washbasin, still on the domestic pet side of the room. Dustin didn't know what it was when they initially entered the room. They arrange the rolling table to be parallel with the x-ray table.

"Okay. Just like last time, try to get as much of your arms as you can under her before we lift to move her," she says.

"Okay," Dustin confirms.

They both lean over to slide their arms under the dog without disturbing her too much. As they proceed to lift her, she lets out a small whimper. Dustin is immediately concerned, but a glance at the doctor's calm face indicates that this is normal for the situation. He calms back down, and they finish moving the dog to the x-ray table.

Melissa turns to Damon, who is standing just inside the saloon doors and says, "Damon, you did everything exactly right. Thank you for your help."

"You're welcome," Damon responds in a shy tone.

"The x-rays don't take long, but it will be about thirty minutes for me to develop them," Melissa says as she turns toward Dustin.

"We can hang around," Dustin responds. "You okay with that bud?" he asks Damon.

"Yeah. Can we take her home when you're done?" Damon quickly asks.

"Woah buddy," Dustin interjects. "This is not our dog. I want to help pay for her treatment, but we're in no position to bring a pet home. We don't even know if Ms. Dora would allow it."

"I bet she would if we told her she's sick and needs a place to rest!" Damon replies a bit louder.

Melissa looks at him and instantly loves how much this little boy cares about this creature he just met tonight. She realizes she can give Dustin an out and calm the boy down at the same time.

"Actually, Damon, she'll need to stay with me for the night so I can work on her. Would you like to come by in the morning to check on her?"

Damon looks up at Dustin with wide eyes. "Can we, Dad?" he says in a much more positive tone.

"Sure buddy. But let's leave the doctor alone to do her work for now. We'll go sit out front while you do the x-rays," Dustin says as he moves his eyes from Damon to Melissa.

"Sounds good," she says.

Dustin opens one side of the saloon doors for Damon to walk through. They head to the front of the clinic where a few chairs are placed near the windows on their left. They sit down, their backs to the window.

"Dad," Damon begins. "We have to take this dog home!"

"Buddy," Dustin sighs. He struggles to conjure the energy to have this discussion right now.

"Come on, Dad. She's a farm dog, and Dora lives on a farm!"

"She doesn't really have a farm anymore buddy," Dustin responds, simultaneously realizing how utterly irrelevant this statement will be to the kid.

"Dad," Damon begins again.

"Listen," Dustin interjects. "Let's see how the x-rays go tonight, and then you heard the doctor. The dog needs to stay here for now."

"Okay, we can ask Dora in the morning!"

Dustin feels a sense of responsibility for the animal. He also begins thinking about how great a distraction the dog would be for Damon. He understands the healing power of having a pet. It wasn't that long ago that he and Holly had lost the two dogs they'd adopted when they were first married. They were both small dogs that liked to sit on their laps while they watched television or read. Dustin is sure the dogs prevented at least a few mental breakdowns for his wife. They had probably helped him, too. Dustin always knew when Holly had a tough day at work, because when she walked through the front door the dogs were the first thing she looked for. She was always a little happier after hugging or petting the dogs. Sometimes this sense of contentment lasted the entire evening. Those were the good days. Sometimes her stress crept back up if they had to discuss money or Damon's school-work. The stress made her extra grumpy, or she just checked out and sort of disappeared from the conversation. There didn't seem to be anything in between. Fortunately, the dogs were always there to help her calm down for bedtime.

Unfortunately, this helped less and less over time after they adopted Damon. Once the dogs died, she didn't have another option for easing her feelings of panic. This is only clear to Dustin in hind-sight. At the time, he handled each situation as it occurred, but couldn't grasp the bigger picture.

He decides he needs to play it safe. They have no idea if the dog will even survive the night. He figures the x-rays will tell them a lot, and he resolves to stay patient as they wait by the front door. If he is to consider taking care of this dog at all, he needs to know what he's getting himself into.

Roughly forty minutes pass. During that time, Dustin and Damon talked about their old dogs and Damon played with some of the pet toys. They sipped the drinks from the ice chest in the truck. Dustin stepped outside the front of the clinic for fresh air. As he reenters, he sees Melissa emerge from the back with a bland look on her face.

Doctors have the best poker faces, he thinks.

"Okay. Mostly good news," she begins. "She has a broken leg. Fortu-nately, it is a clean break and should heal with no problem. I'll have to put a cast on it, though. She also has one broken rib. Amazing it's not more. That will heal okay too, but she won't be able to move around much in the meantime."

"How long?" Dustin asks.

"Why, you thinkin' about taking her?" Melissa asks with a wry smile.

Dustin purses his lips and thinks for a second. "Well. I just need to know what she has ahead of her."

They both crack half a smile. Melissa decides not to press him on it, and Dustin realizes he isn't fooling anyone with his coy demeanor and wordplay.

"Well, thanks for hanging out," Melissa continues. "I was able to reach my assistant on the phone; she's headed over to help me set the leg and put on the cast. You guys can go if you want. The dog's gonna be fine."

"Yeah, I don't think I'd be much help with that anyway," Dustin responds with a slight grin. "Okay, well, I guess we'll be by in the morning. I promised him we'd check on her."

"Okay," Melissa responds.

"Okay," Dustin says, and then pauses. "Well, it was nice to meet you," he continues as he holds up his hand to wave awkwardly.

"Nice to meet you too. See you in the morning," Melissa replies.

Dustin finally turns to make his way back to the front and then realizes that Damon was nearby for the entire exchange. "Okay Damon, time to go."

"She's gonna be okay Dad?" asks Damon as they head for the door.

Dustin wraps his right arm around Damon's shoulder and says, "Yeah buddy, I think she'll be fine."

Home

The next morning, as Damon wakes up in the front room of their house, he is so excited he can hardly contain it. His first thought is to run into the only other room in their shack to wake Dustin.

"Dad," Damon whispers excitedly. "It's time to go back to the vet."

"What?" Dustin responds in a groggy voice.

"The dog, Dad. We need to go check on it. We gotta ask her if she can stay here."

Dustin, extremely confused by Damon's broken narrative and overuse of pronouns, briefly thinks about how terribly he slept last night.

Then he remembers. *The dog.*

"Buddy. I told you the dog might not get to stay here. It might not be ready to leave the doctor today, anyway. Don't get too excited about this," Dustin finishes and rolls onto his side.

Damon visibly controls his tone.

"Dad, I know. I just want to check on her like you said we would."

He is attempting to demonstrate for Dustin that he doesn't have his hopes too high, even though he does.

Dustin sighs and rolls over to look directly at Damon. With his head on his pillow, he says, "Okay buddy. Just let me get up, okay? And we need to eat breakfast first."

"Okay!" Damon says as he begins turning around to exit the room. "And go wash up and brush your teeth!"

After stretching his arms a bit, Dustin knows he won't be able to go back to sleep.

Too much to do. Unpacking, need to feed Damon, need to follow-up on that job. I hope I haven't backed myself into a corner with this dog situation, Dustin thinks. *I wonder what Holly is doing.*

Dustin still isn't completely sure what it means to give her some space, but that's what Holly asked for. He figures she just needs a break, some time to decompress and realize that things are never as bad as they seem. This has always been the problem, though. To Holly, everything seems worse than it is. He thinks about what she would do with this dog situation and quietly laughs.

Bringing a dog home is just about the only thing she would never worry about, he realizes.

Oddly, this gives Dustin a positive feeling that pushes him to get out of bed and follow through on his promise to Damon.

Holly would take Damon to check on the dog if she were here.

After taking a quick shower and brushing his teeth, Dustin moves into the front of the house. He looks out the front window to see Damon playing. He has a stick, and he is clearly talking to himself and poking things with it.

This is perfect, Dustin thinks. *This is exactly what a little boy should be doing with his time.*

He turns his attention to the few boxes they brought with them.

I'm sure I put a coffee maker in one of these, he thinks as he sifts through the largest box.

After removing other kitchen utensils and the random toys and books Damon had hurriedly packed, he finally sees the small coffee maker. It only makes four cups, but it was really the perfect size for the tiny kitchenette they have. He'd also brought some bread with them. There was already a toaster on the counter, so Dustin decides to give it a try.

It works! Dry wheat toast and black coffee for me. I better figure out something else for Damon though, he thinks. *The doughnut shop in town. Sheesh, what a typical dad breakfast.*

Dustin unpacks and puts away a few more things while sipping his coffee. Damon finally makes his way back into the house and asks Dustin if he is ready to go.

"Let me just finish my coffee, okay buddy?

"Okay," Damon responds.

"You can brush your teeth while you're waiting for me," Dustin says.

"Dad, I already…" Damon begins.

Dustin quickly cuts him off, "Don't man…I checked your tooth-brush. It's dry as a bone."

Damon ducks his head, glancing up shamefully at his dad.

"I know you're excited about today, but you can't lie to me, buddy," Dustin says as he rubs Damon's shoulder.

"Okay," Damon says as he slowly moves toward the bathroom, his head still down.

Dustin puts his boots on and gives Damon a kiss on his head just before they head out the door.

As they step off the small wooden stoop Damon says, "We're going to go ask Dora, right Dad?"

"Buddy, it's kind of early, and I don't want to bother her if she is still sleeping," Dustin responds as they near the corner of Dora's house.

"You'll never be up before me," a voice says from the other side of the corner. It startles Dustin a little. They peek around the corner of the house to see Dora plucking some small weeds from the flower bed near her porch.

"Now what did you want to ask me?" she says.

"Can we bring a dog here?" Damon blurts out.

"Damon …" Dustin begins.

"A dog?" Dora replies to Damon as if Dustin isn't standing there. She sets down the small shovel in her hand and begins taking off her worn-out gardening gloves. She looks toward the front lawn of the house in silence, almost as if she is trying to envision a dog playing in that space. She holds both gloves in one hand, stands up, and places her right fist on her hip.

"Is it okay with your dad?" she says to Damon.

"I think so!" he responds.

"You think so? You gonna feed it and clean up after it?" she asks.

"Well, yeah."

"Well yeah?" she echoes.

She stares at the boy, almost as if she is trying to look into his eyes to see if he is genuine in his commitment. Dustin quickly realizes what a good influence Dora will be on Damon if they stick around long enough. She is a person of few words, but Dustin has a feeling that she knows more and thinks more than she lets on. This is a form of wisdom he might benefit from as well.

"Okay," she says finally.

"Really?" Damon says.

"Well, you just told me you're going to take care of it, didn't you?" she replies.

"Thanks!" Damon shouts as he begins running toward the truck as if there isn't a moment to waste.

"Wow, uh, thanks," Dustin says.

"Boys need responsibility, don't they?" Dora says, as if she's referring to them both and not just Damon.

"Sure. Right. Well, we're not yet sure what we're getting ourselves into here. We need to see if the vet says the dog will be okay," Dustin says, probing to see if Dora wants more details about the situation. "Okay. Well, there are some dog dishes on the back porch if you need 'em," she says curtly as she kneels back down to work on the garden.

"Ah. Okay, thanks," Dustin realizes he's being dismissed. "We're heading into town. Do you need anything?"

"No thanks. I'm fine," Dora responds, her head down as she continues picking at the soil.

Dustin realizes it's probably been a long time since Dora had to ask anyone for anything, and she's not about to start now.

"Okay. See you in a bit," Dustin says as he heads to the truck.

Dustin parks the truck directly in front of the vet again. This time, though, the truck is facing the correct way. Dustin checks his mirror for oncoming cars, then opens the door when it is clear. He walks around the truck and helps Damon close the truck door on the passenger side. It is Saturday, so the clinic is not as busy with farm animals as a weekday would be. Dustin can see a few people inside through the front window. When he opens the front door, he notices that Melissa has an assistant who runs the front desk for her. It's a girl who doesn't look much older than a teenager. Dustin figures it's probably a local high school student. He begins walking toward the back of the clinic with the intent of asking this person to let Melissa know that they're there. Just as he steps behind the person currently at the counter with the cash register, Melissa emerges form the back with a small animal carrier, looks over at one of the customers shopping, and says in a loud voice, "Nance, Noodle is ready to go." She sets the carrier on the other counter. She then sets a small bottle of prescription medication next to it. As she waits for Nancy to come to the back counter, she scans the shop and realizes that Dustin and Damon are there.

"You guys came back," she says to Dustin.

"Yep," Dustin quickly replies, not wanting to interrupt her interaction with the other customers. Melissa smiles gently and looks down at the counter, then up at Nancy.

"Well, I can't tell if she was bit or if she got her leg stuck in something. She'll be fine though. Just give her this antibiotic once a day with a meal," Melissa says, pointing at the white label on the prescription bottle.

"Thanks so much, Melissa," Nancy says as she steps into Dustin's spot in the other line.

"That only took ten minutes Rachel. Just ring her up for the medicine, okay?" Melissa says as she turns her gaze toward Dustin.

"Okay," Rachel responds.

Dustin begins making his way to the other counter where the doctor is, and he says, "Helping out the townsfolk for free again?"

Melissa smiles, takes a deep breath, looks down at the counter, and then answers, "Funny. I should make you pay for the girl you brought in last night for saying that."

Dustin chuckles.

"Well, how is she?" he then says.

"Why don't you guys come back and see for yourself," she says in a happier tone while looking at Damon. Damon smiles a big smile and then nods his head quickly.

They proceed between the two counters and through the saloon doors to the back room with the examination tables. Dustin hadn't noticed it the night before, but behind the exam room was a small kennel with stacked cages for animals to stay in while recovering. Melissa steps inside the room and Dustin can hear her unlatching one of the cages. A few seconds later, she emerges with the dog on a rolling cart. The dog is sitting up nervously, and when it sees Dustin and Damon it tries to move its paws a little. It quickly realizes it has nowhere to go and then, upon catching their scents, seems to find a level of comfort with the situation. Clearly tired from the night before, she gently sets her head back down on the cart just as it rolls to a stop in front of Dustin and Damon.

Dustin sees a small cast on her leg and says, "She seems pretty good."

"She's doing well, all things considered," Melissa replies.

Damon reaches out to pet the dog, who only moves her eyes to look at him.

"Just don't pet her belly, hon," Melissa says. "We don't want to make her rib hurt any more than it does already."

"Okay," Damon says as he begins scratching her neck slowly and carefully.

Dustin can see the look in Damon's eyes.

He's already in love with the dog. I guess it's good that he wants to help her, Dustin thinks.

He can tell that Melissa is seeing the same thing.

"Well, we have permission to bring her home with us," he says, giving the dog a quick scratch behind the ear. "Can she walk?"

"Damon, I'm going to show your dad something over here on the x-ray charts, okay? Just be careful petting her."

"Okay," he says quietly, clearly still enamored with the dog.

The two of them walk over to the wall with a light display and begin looking at the x-rays.

"It's still the same as I told you last night. You can see the cast on the leg, and there is the one broken rib," the doctor begins.

"Okay," Dustin responds.

"After you left last night, though, I ran an MRI on her, and I found something else."

"Oh. Okay. What is it?" Dustin says.

"Well, it's not from the accident. Basically, she has a tumor near her spleen. It is a form of cancer that is relatively common in dogs. The problem is that hers is at an advanced stage," she says in a somber tone.

"Okay, but what does that mean?" Dustin says.

"It means she won't live for much more than three to six months," Melissa says.

"Ah. Oh man," Dustin sighs as he looks over at Damon petting the dog.

Damon hadn't lost his mom yet, but he misses her. Making a new friend like this dog and then losing it so quickly is not something Dustin planned for when he brought Damon here.

"So, what happens if we don't take her?" Dustin finally says.

"Well, she doesn't have a home. I would probably go ahead and put her to sleep," Melissa says with a tear beginning to roll down her cheek. "I could let her live here for a bit, but I can't get attached to her. I've been down that road before."

Dustin can tell she is holding back more tears. Not so much because of this dog's situation, but because of something she went through in the past. He realizes that everyone is going to be sad, no matter what they do.

Dustin looks at the dog and wonders, *Do you have a few more happy months left in you?*

He is suddenly feeling the weight of everyone in the room's feelings.

Melissa wipes her face with her left hand. She looks at her pen to make sure it is clicked closed then puts it back into the pocket of her lab coat.

"I know this is a tough situation, and I don't expect anything from you guys. Why don't you hang out back here for a few minutes and decide what you want to do?"

"Okay," Dustin responds.

"I have to do this all the time, so don't worry about that part of it," she says as she snaps back into professional doctor mode.

"Okay. Thanks," Dustin repeats.

Melissa heads through the saloon doors to the front to talk to other customers. Dustin turns around and stares at the x-rays as if he is going to suddenly know how to read them and get some sort of answer from them. Not sure what to do next, he turns back around and looks at Damon. He quickly resolves not to overthink the situation.

What does Damon need now? he asks himself. He can't shake the feeling that Damon needs a pal right now. *He needs a partner in crime for the summer. He doesn't yet have any friends here. This is what he needs right now. He'll learn from this too.*

Dustin walks toward Damon and says, "Well, how's she doing buddy?"

"I think she's okay Dad. She licked my hand!"

Dustin cracks a smile, "Ha, that's funny."

Damon looks up at Dustin and doesn't have to ask the question. Dustin can see it on his face.

"You think you can take care of her?" he asks Damon.

"Yes, Dad!"

"She's going to need a lot of extra help for the next few days. You know that, right?"

"Well, yeah Dad. What else do I have to do?"

"That's true," Dustin says, dragging out the interaction a little more.

He takes a deep breath. Damon is soothing the dog and already bonding with her.

"Okay man," Dustin finally says as he lets out a deep breath.

Damon turns around carefully, and says, "Dad, I promise I'll take care of her."

Dustin is impressed with this display of maturity. Instead of getting excited and running out to the truck, leaving everyone else to deal with the dog, Damon seems to genuinely understand how much work he has ahead of him.

He knows that the work begins now, Dustin thinks.

As Dustin drives the truck into the alley behind the clinic, he sees Melissa opening the back door. Dustin pulls up next to the door, shifts the truck into park, and turns the engine off. As he exits the truck, Melissa is helping Damon push the cart with the dog on it through the door. Dustin walks around the truck and grabs a sleeping bag from the passenger side of the truck bed.

"Is this enough to get her home?" he asks Melissa.

"Yes. Obviously, be careful and watch out for bumps in the road," she responds.

Dustin half smiles back at her while unzipping the sleeping bag.

The table of the stainless-steel cart is just a few inches lower than the open tailgate. Damon clearly wants to help move the dog, but knows to stay out of the way while the adults do the heavy lifting.

The dog seems to be very comfortable with the situation, Dustin thinks. *I think we're doing the right thing here.*

Dustin places the sleeping bag on the tailgate. He and Melissa lift the dog onto it, and then they slide the sleeping bag with the dog on it into the truck bed. Dustin closes the tailgate gently and looks at the dog to ensure she is comfortable.

"She's pretty well knocked up on meds right now," Melissa says. "I'll get you some food to take with you. You can hide the medication in the food. She should have a pretty big appetite by tonight. It's an antibiotic plus something for the pain."

"Okay," Dustin says as he nods his head.

"She should be able to go to the bathroom on her own tomorrow. Don't be alarmed if there is some slight whimpering. She still has a lot of healing to do," Melissa concludes.

"Okay, well, thanks for everything," Dustin says slowly and awkwardly.

He's not sure if a handshake is appropriate, or maybe a hug given what they've all been through together. He extends his hand.

The doctor furrows her brow, and says in a no-nonsense tone, "How about a hug?"

She extends her arms slightly.

"Oh, right," Dustin responds as if he wasn't already thinking it.

They exchange a quick hug. Melissa turns to Damon.

"You take care of her, okay Damon?"

"I will," Damon responds. He then holds up a small cloth sack and says, "Here."

"What's this?" Melissa asks.

"It's to pay for the dog food," he says as he extends his arm with the sack further.

Melissa takes the purple bag, which is cinched closed with gold colored string. She opens it and reaches inside. She pulls her hand out and it is full of random coins, a dollar bill, and some fake plastic gemstones Damon had collected. Melissa smiles and looks at Dustin. He meets her eyes and covers his mouth with his hand so Damon doesn't realize how cute they think he is right now.

He's trying to be a responsible young man right now. This is awesome, Dustin thinks.

"Oh, that's okay honey," Melissa finally says. "You keep this. You helped your dad and me save this dog. How about I buy the food this time, and you take me to the drive-in sometime? What do you think?"

"Okay," Damon responds in an awkward, shy tone. He reaches out and takes the sack back.

"You sure we don't owe you anything for all this?" Dustin says.

"You're taking care of her. That is enough," Melissa says firmly.

Dustin silently acknowledges this with a nod and turns to get in his truck.

As Dustin and Damon slam the truck doors closed, Melissa approaches the window and says, "Let me know how she's doin' in a few days, okay?"

"You bet. Thanks again," Dustin says as he starts the truck and shifts into drive.

They slowly drive down the alleyway to head home with the new family member.

Junk

Sunday morning Dustin needs to meet a construction foreman about work for Monday. If it works out, he'll start tomorrow and have work for weeks. He won't be gone long, and Dora agrees to keep an eye on Damon for him. Dustin feeds Damon, quickly checks on the dog, and then leaves for his meeting.

We really need to give this dog a name, he thinks.

As he's walking to the truck, he can hear Damon talking to the dog about everything they were going to do that day. He trusts Damon to be careful with the dog, and Dora is already out on her porch sweeping, so she can easily check on them.

Dustin waves to her and says, "Good morning."

Dora looks up from her sweeping and says, "Mornin.'"

He quickly realizes that he feels a sense of home in this place. Though he knows it is temporary, he has a feeling of contentment that usually only comes with familiarity.

It feels good. It feels safe, he thinks.

Dustin parks his truck next to a mobile office building situated in a neighborhood that is being rebuilt. He steps out of the truck and surveys the area. The entire neighborhood had burned down. He hadn't been in the middle of the devastation like this before. The amount of work to rebuild this part of the town immediately feels overwhelming. He quickly understands why his contact, Jarrett, is working on a Sunday.

Dustin climbs the metal steps up to the small landing outside the mobile office door. He knocks gently. A voice from inside energetically says, "Come in!" The man inside seems distracted, almost annoyed. Dustin enters through the flimsy door and sees a heavy-set man with dark but graying hair facing the corner of the room. Dustin looks to his left and sees a drafting table with blueprints. Next to it is an L-shaped corner desk under a window looking outside. To his right is an oval-shaped table with chairs for meeting. He assumes this is Jarrett sitting at the L-shaped desk.

"Hi, I'm Dustin Harris. I think we spoke on the phone about me working this week?"

"Dustin! Hi, I'm Jarrett," the man responds, spinning around in his chair to extend a hand to shake. "You have your own tools?"

Dustin shakes his hand, realizes how little time this guy has for pleasantries, and quickly answers, "Yes, I have all the basics."

"Good enough," Jarrett quickly shoots back. "I really hope you know what you're doing. I got more dopes with hammers than I need right now. I need someone who can keep them from doing something dumb. You think you can help me with that?"

"Sure. I've built numerous houses, and done some commercial stuff too," Dustin says.

"Great. Okay. You can start tomorrow?" Jarrett asks.

"I can," Dustin responds.

"Come with me," Jarrett directs Dustin.

Dustin follows him out of the trailer and down the metal steps. They walk over to a group of five homes around a cul-de-sac.

"This is what you'll be working on tomorrow," Jarrett says while pointing at the homes with a rolled-up set of blueprints. "Frames are mostly done, and we need to get the sheeting done in the next two days so the roofing guys can start."

Dustin is taken aback at the amount of work this guy is expecting in the next couple of days.

Those roof lines are complicated, which means a lot of cuts to make in the plywood sheets, he thinks.

Jarrett sees the look of concern on Dustin's face.

"It's a lot of work, my man," he says to address Dustin's silence. "See that house over there?" he says, again pointing with the blueprints.

Dustin looks in that direction.

"That's my place. So, you better take extra care on that one," he says with a wry smile.

Dustin is speechless.

This guy isn't just rebuilding his community. He's rebuilding his life.

Dustin just met him and figures it's too soon to ask personal questions about the health and safety of this family. He then realizes a sense of conviction that he doesn't have on most jobs.

It's always fun to see things you've built when driving around the town you live in. But this is different, he thinks.

"So, seven tomorrow morning?" Jarrett asks.

"You bet," Dustin answers. "I'll be here."

"Good man," Jarrett says as he shakes Dustin's hand for a second time.

They agree on Dustin's hourly rate and work out some details and paperwork before Dustin heads back to Dora's.

As Dustin approaches Dora's house, he sees Damon by some of the farming equipment that lays around the yard like a rusty old museum. Damon has something in his hand, and when he sees Dustin he turns and runs toward their house.

Oh man, what is he up to now? Dustin thinks.

He exits the truck and Dora catches his attention.

She puts some tools into her shed and says, "Damon was asking some questions."

"Oh. About what?" Dustin asks.

"You know. Everything," Dora responds somewhat sarcastically.

Dustin realizes he's put off explaining to Damon why they here.

"Ah. I gotcha," Dustin replies, embarrassed.

"You know, that porch swing is a great place for a small talk," says Dora.

Dustin looks at the porch swing, and then back at Dora.

"Thanks," Dustin says as he nods his head and turns to go check on Damon.

As Dustin walks around the main house and the smaller back house comes into view, he can see Damon's back as Damon tinkers with something. Dustin doesn't see the dog anywhere, and immediately begins questioning Damon.

"Damon, where's the dog?" he asks sharply.

Before turning around, Damon says "Look what I made Dad!"

Damon turns and moves out of the way with a look of pride on his face. Dustin can now see the dog, and the contraption Damon built. It is essentially an old wheelbarrow with some tattered blankets and pillows in the bowl. The dog is lying in there, her head down. She shifts her eyes up to look at Dustin, almost as if to say *Please get me out of here*.

"Check this out," Damon says. "This is so she can drink water when we're going somewhere!"

Damon grabs a metal bowl attached to a metal bar on a hinge. He had attached the hinge to the wheelbarrow with a c-clamp so that he can move the water bowl close to the dog or away from the dog. Of course, this invention has no practical need for the hinge, but it is certainly holding up the bowl of water so the dog can drink from it. Dustin feels a sense of pride at his son's ingenuity. He'd clearly spent the past hour or so thinking about how to best care for the dog. Dustin then has a sudden realization.

"How'd you get her into the wheelbarrow, buddy?"

"I parked it right by the porch and she got in!" Damon responds with excitement.

"You mean she was able to walk today?"

"Ya, just a little bit. She went pee-pee over there," he says as he points to a wet mark on the porch.

"Oh good!" Dustin exclaims. "What else did you guys do?"

"Nuthin'. She just mostly lays there," Damon responds.

Dustin squats down to pet the dog and says, "Yeah. She still needs a lot of rest, buddy."

He pauses silently for a few seconds

He then says, "What about a name?"

"I think we should name her Holly, since Mom isn't here," Damon says.

So many thoughts flood Dustin's mind.

He must be missing his mom already. Holly isn't a terrible name for a dog. Why not let him name the dog after his mom? I can't think of any better names.

Rather than pick a name immediately, he decides it is time for that small talk Dora mentioned.

"Let's go sit on the porch for a few minutes."

"You think she'll be okay?" Damon says as he gestures toward the dog.

Dustin looks at her tired eyes and says, "Yeah. I don't think she's going anywhere."

They sit on the porch swing and Dustin uses his foot to lightly swing them.

"You miss your mom?" he begins.

"Yeah. I know it's only been one day, but I don't understand why she isn't here with us. Like, how long are we gonna be here?"

"Well, buddy, your mom needs some time to focus on herself. We're just here so she can concentrate on her mental health without us distracting her."

"What does that even mean?" Damon says with a puzzled look.

Dustin stares off into the trees for a moment.

"You know how you go to the doctor to fix your body when you get hurt or sick?"

"Yeah."

"Well, sometimes people need to do the same thing for their brain, for their mind."

"Mom's going to a brain doctor?"

"Sort of. They can help her understand why she is extra tired sometimes. Why she is frustrated a lot. Stuff like that. So she can be happier when we do stuff together, you know?"

Damon mimics his father and stares off into the trees.

"She does yell sometimes," Damon says.

"Yeah. Well, Mom and I both need to work on that," says Dustin as he looks at the floor of the porch. He remembers that he needs to work on himself too.

After a few moments of silence, Damon, apparently satisfied with the conversation, changes the subject.

"What about the dog's name? Can we call her Holly?"

"Well, we don't want Mom to think we're trying to replace her, do we?" Dustin replies. "What about Mom's middle name?"

"Hope?" Damon asks.

"Yeah. I think that could be a good name for a stray dog," Dustin says.

"Huh. Okay. I guess we can do that," Damon finally says. "Mom's going to think that's funny when she meets her though, don't you think?"

"Yeah. Probably," Dustin says with a smile. He wraps one arm around Damon to hug him, again staring out at the forest.

Not Today

The next day, Monday morning, it is time for Dustin to go to work. Not one for planning ahead very well, he is suddenly worried about Damon.

It's summertime, but what is Damon going to do all day? Dora's watching him, but does she really know what she's committed to? he thinks.

As Dustin completes his thought, he walks out of his bedroom to see Damon already up and checking on the dog.

Ah, that's what he'll do all day.

Dustin is happy to see what a caring little guy Damon is becoming.

After shoveling down some quick breakfast, Dustin says bye to Damon and walks out of the house. Once around the corner of the main house, he finds Dora in the front yard having already started her day. She was again working in the garden.

"Good morning," Dustin says happily.

"Good morning," she replies.

"Hey, I just wanted to double-check that you're okay watching him while I work," Dustin begins.

"You going to help rebuild homes?" she says, cutting him off.

She continues to prepare her tools and never looks directly at Dustin.

"Yes, that's exactly what I'll be working on today."

"Then yes, I am happy to keep an eye on him ... and the dog," she says with a sideways look at Dustin, eyebrows raised.

"About that," Dustin begins.

Dora cuts him off.

"Don't you think you need to get going, or you'll be late for your first day? Go on, before I change my mind," she says as she finally stops and looks directly at him.

Dustin smiles a small smile and says, "Right ... yes, of course. Thank you."

She winks at him quickly, and they turn away from each other. Dustin heads to the truck and, as he walks toward it, he glances back at Dora who is already working in her garden again.

Damon is just off the front stoop of the house, trying to coax Hope into the wheelbarrow. She's not going for it today. It is clear to Damon that Hope is determined to walk more today than yesterday. Suddenly he's worried about how he'll keep her nearby. Dora's property has no true fence around it, and a momentary lapse could allow her to be lost in the woods around the house. Damon's sole mission becomes finding rope to act as a leash. He heads toward a small utility shed near his house and opens the creaky, dilapidated door to see what's inside. For Damon, it is a wonderland of cool-looking stuff: tools, rusty parts from farm equipment, and small shelves lined with jars and coffee cans full of nails and screws.

There's got to be some rope in here, he thinks.

Hope gingerly walks over to Damon at the shed. The cast on her front leg prevents her from bending it. To walk, she must awkwardly swing the leg in a semi-circle before touching it to the ground for each step. She finally makes it to the shed and briefly looks in and sniffs to see what Damon is up to. Her black and white fur is matted from all the laying around she's been doing. She instinctively begins to roll her head and body to shake it out, but the pain from the healing rib stops her mid roll. She's not ready to shake out her coat just yet, still too much pain in her midsection. She quickly loses interest in what Damon is doing and turns away from the shed to look around. She squints her eyes a little with the sun in her face, but the warmth feels good. She sees the main house, the side of the porch, and the front lawn with the rusting farm equipment scattered around it. She feels safe, but also knows this isn't her home.

Home. I need to go home, she feels.

She begins walking away from the shed and toward the front lawn of the house. She's moving very slowly, but it still feels good to be moving toward home. As she passes the side of the porch and enters the front yard, Dora catches her in her peripheral vision and begins watching. Dora knows the dog isn't going to go far with the cast on her leg and decides this is a good time to test Damon's sense of responsibility. Hope steps onto the gravel driveway, which is shaped like a teardrop, in front of the house. The gravel feels quite different from the mix of soft dirt and grass she walked on to get there. Walking is becoming more difficult, and the coarse gravel adds a tiny pinch of pain to the leg and the rib with every step. She is determined to keep moving toward home though.

Damon sifts through the old wooden fruit crates to find something he can use for a leash. He sees some baling wire, but figures that won't work very well. He tries, but can't bend it with his bare hands. In the next crate, under the one with the baling wire, he finds a rusty metal stake with a hole at the top. He lifts it up to the light shining through the only window in the shed.

Yeah. I can tie a rope to this, he thinks.

He sets it on the ground next to him and says to Hope, "We gotta make sure you don't run off."

He has no idea Hope has already wandered off.

Dora watches from her gardening hutch on the other side of the house. She can see Hope meandering down the gravel drive. She figures she'll give Damon another minute or two to realize the dog is leaving. Dora notices Hope gradually slow down as she wanders further away from the house. As Hope approaches the border between grassy lawn and forest, she slows to a stop.

Guess I won't have to chase her after all, Dora thinks.

She casually looks toward the other side of the house to see if Damon has realized that the dog has wandered away. Still no sign of the boy.

Hope feels tired. The path of the driveway is clear, but the wall of trees and brush feels overwhelming to the recovering dog. Still no scent of her home either. She is driven to keep moving forward, but her body is not cooperating; not today. She decides it's best to retreat to the safety of the boy, the soft bed, and the wheelbarrow. She turns around and looks at the main house. She gently sniffs the air and takes a deep breath. She slowly makes her way off the coarse gravel drive to the safety of the grassy lawn. She awkwardly hobbles in a circle two or three times to tamp down the grass and then gingerly lays in it.

Dora sees Hope lay down in front of the main house and thinks, *That dog looks like she's lived here for years.*

She cracks a small smile and turns her attention back to the clay flower pots and soil she is working with.

Damon finishes sifting through the crates and stands up from his knees. More light is shining through the single window of the shed and dust is floating through it. Damon brushes his hands together to knock off the rust and dirt, and then looks up at some things hanging on the wall.

There it is, he thinks. *Some rope!*

He steps on an upside-down milk crate and reaches up for the rope.

"Okay, Hope," he begins as he grabs the rope off the wall and turns toward the door.

He quickly realizes the dog is not there anymore and feels the dread of messing up on his first day watching the dog.

"Hope?"

He darts out of the shed and looks at the stoop to see no sign of her at his house. With the fraying brown rope in his hand, he decides to head to the front of the main house to look for the dog. As he rounds the corner of the front porch she comes into view. There she is, laying calmly on the lawn enjoying the sun and the breeze while Damon is about to have a panic attack.

There you are, Damon thinks as he breathes a massive sigh of relief.

He looks over and sees Dora minding her own business in the garden. He figures she isn't paying attention. Dora, meanwhile, feels confident the boy has learned a lesson this day.

I hope he has to learn that lesson only once, she thinks as she scratches at the garden soil.

Damon walks over to Hope and decides to just sit on the grass with her. He looks at the rope in his hand and sets it on the ground.

Well, maybe I won't need this after all, he thinks.

Damon pets the dog gently and she takes a deep breath, stares off into the trees, and relaxes.

That night, on his way home from the job site, Dustin decides it might be time to call his wife. On his way through town, he remembers there is a pay phone across the street from the veterinary clinic.

I wonder what Holly's doing right now? he thinks.

He finds a place to park and eases his truck into it. He turns off the engine, but leaves the keys in the ignition.

With his hands back on the steering wheel he thinks, *She doesn't want to talk to me right now.*

He suddenly feels nervous.

Why am I nervous about calling my own wife?

Dustin realizes that his last few interactions with her were incredibly stressful. That stress was only one of the things that led to needing a break. Holly was constantly overwhelmed by her own feelings. Dustin felt like there was never any room to tell her how he was feeling. There was no room to tell her if something was bothering him, even if that something wasn't her. It could have been something at work or struggles with fatherhood, but how could he lay his problems on someone who constantly feels overwhelmed?

Dustin looks down at his hands and his knuckles are white from gripping the steering wheel so tightly.

Jesus. No wonder I'm so tense, he thinks as he removes his hands from the wheel and shakes them out.

He takes a deep breath and then lets it out as he stares through the window at the payphone.

I better go check on Damon, he thinks as he places his fingers back on the keys dangling from the ignition.

He pauses for a second, and then cranks the engine back up.

I need to call her. But not today, he thinks as he begins driving home.

Checkup

Over the next two weeks, Dustin and Damon continue to settle into their new home and town. Work is going well, Hope the dog is healing nicely, and Dora insists that Damon is very easy to watch. He is also helpful around the property. Occasionally he tries to fix something only to make it worse, but Dustin is proud of Damon's ingenuity and attempts at being helpful. Dora is much more patient than Dustin expected, and she insists that Damon is more help than harm. Every time Dustin thinks about how much Dora is doing for them, for free, it pushes him to work harder to rebuild her community. He can't help but think she is getting something else out of the deal though. She must have been lonely, at least sometimes, before they moved in. She'd never say it aloud, but Dustin thinks she is enjoying their company.

On a Thursday, Dustin leaves work a little early so he and Damon can take Hope to the vet for a checkup. This is the first time Hope will ride in the back of the truck since they first brought her home from the vet. She seems right at home in the truck bed, causing Dustin to wonder again about her background and where she'd come from. Damon is already in the passenger seat of the truck as Dustin jumps in.

"Ready buddy?" he asks Damon.

"Yeah. I just hope the doctor says she's okay," he responds in a worried tone.

"Yeah, me too. This is just routine though, bub. It's mostly so we can see if she doesn't need the meds anymore. Okay?"

"Okay," Damon responds, unconvinced.

They're again able to park directly in front of the clinic on the street. After exiting the truck, Dustin walks to the back of the truck bed and opens the tailgate. Hope awkwardly stands up on her cast and hobbles to the back of the truck. Seeing her recognize their location, Dustin begins to realize how intelligent this dog is.

So this is how you survived on your own this whole time, huh girl? he thinks as he gently lifts her up and sets her on the sidewalk next to the truck.

"Don't forget the leash, Dad," Damon says as he rushes over to them.

"Go ahead and put it on her, buddy," Dustin responds.

Damon secures his homemade leash on Hope and begins leading her up the entry to the door of the clinic.

Melissa is in the back of the clinic by the counters when she sees them approaching through the front windows. Her dark hair is in a ponytail as usual, and she is excited to find out how the dog is doing.

"Hi, you guys," she says as they walk up the center aisle of the clinic. "Wow, she's really walking well!"

"Yeah, even with the cast she can run a little bit!" Damon responds.

"Great. You're not letting her get too crazy though, right?" Melissa responds.

"Right. I even made a rope leash to keep her nearby," says Damon.

"So, I guess you guys are keeping her," she says quietly to Dustin.

"Yes. She's super smart, and fitting in over at Dora's," Dustin says. "We even gave her a name."

"I was wondering about that. What is it?" says Melissa.

"Hope!" Damon exclaims. "Just like my mom!"

"I bet that was your idea." Melissa says to him.

Damon smiles enthusiastically and Dustin says, "Well, it's Holly's middle name."

"Oh, is that your wife?" Melissa asks.

"Right. She's not here though. We're on a bit of a boys' adventure away for a while."

Dustin isn't sure why he just spilled those details to Melissa, except that he senses a bit of a friendship developing. Oddly, he also senses a bit of disappointment from Melissa after he tells her he's married. It occurs to him that he doesn't have a ring on. As a carpenter, he hasn't worn his wedding ring in years.

Melissa abruptly flips back into doctor mode. "Okay. Well, let's take her in the back and check her out." Her white lab coat swings around a bit as she turns to go in the back.

They guide the dog past the counters, and as Melissa holds one of the saloon-style doors open, they pass into the back of the clinic. Dustin lifts the dog onto the stainless-steel table. As he does this, Melissa notices the dog doesn't seem to be uncomfortable at all.

"Wow," she says.

"What?" Dustin says.

"That didn't seem to bother her at all. Her ribs must be almost healed up. You're a strong one, aren't you, girl." Melissa says as she looks at Hope's eyes with a small flashlight.

"How long until we can take the cast off?" Dustin asks.

"Should be another couple of weeks," she says as she feels around Hope's midsection with her hands. She then pulls out her stethoscope and listens to the dog's breathing and heartbeat.

"Did you finish the antibiotics?"

"Yeah. I have the bottle here if she needs more," Dustin responds.

"That's okay, she's done with those. What about the pain medicine?"

"She hasn't seemed to need it for a few days. I can't believe how well she gets around. It's almost as if she's on a mission to get well. I think she's gonna be a real handful when that cast comes off," Dustin says with small laugh.

"Well, it seems like she's doing great. Is she going potty regularly, Damon?"

Damon, slightly embarrassed, says, "Yes. My dad makes me pick it up." He then looks at Dustin with a grimace.

"Alright. I think that's it then," says Melissa as she lifts the dog off the table.

"Awesome," Dustin responds.

Damon walks ahead with the dog and they go through the saloon doors. Dustin stays back to talk to Melissa privately.

"Hey. What about the cancer?" Dustin asks in a somber tone.

"Well, there's not much to do until she shows some other symptoms. Just watch if she becomes lethargic, whether she eats or not, and if she has trouble going potty. Keep an eye on her stool," says Melissa in a more serious tone. "It could be a while. So, just enjoy her company while you can, you know?"

"Yeah. Okay. I don't know what I thought you were going to tell me," Dustin says with a touch of embarrassment.

"That's okay," Melissa responds. "I am her doctor, after all," she says in a silly tone.

They look at each other for a moment as Dustin silently nods his head in agreement. Melissa finally breaks the silence by asking if they need any dog food.

"Yes. I was going to get some on the way home."

"Just take some from the front," says Melissa. "It's on me."

"You don't have to do …," Dustin begins, before being interrupted by the doctor.

"Would you just take it?" she says.

Dustin smiles. "Yes. Thank you."

They continue making their way to the front, and Dustin heads for the bags of dog food stacked up along the wall.

"Take the blue and white one," Melissa says across the room.

"Okay," Dustin says as he leans over to pick up the bag. "You ready, buddy?"

"Yep, we're ready," Damon responds.

They turn and say goodbye to Melissa, then leave through the clinic's front door.

She's Got My Number

The next day is Friday, and Dustin is looking forward to the weekend. He is getting used to nine- and ten-hour workdays. It feels like everyone at the job site is pushing to get people back into their homes as fast as possible. Obviously, the money and overtime pay are good, but that isn't the motivation for these guys. Dustin really feels like he is part of a team, and they're all pushing each other forward. He is just about to finish the sheetrock on a wall inside the house he is working in, when Jarrett sticks his head in the room to tell Dustin to take a lunch break.

"Come on, guys. Put the tools down and go eat. The last thing I need is one of you goofs passing out in here," Jarrett says.

Jarrett was maniacal about the work, but Dustin can tell he is a very caring person with a stern exterior. It is clear to Dustin that the man still hasn't recovered from the loss of his own home and is hiding from it by working a lot. It is hard to fault him for this, but Dustin wonders if Jarrett should worry more about himself burning out and less about the work crew.

As Jarrett turns to walk out of the house, Dustin sets his screw gun on the floor and jogs to catch up with him.

"Hey, Jarret?" Dustin says while exhaling a deep breath.

"Yeah, bud," Jarret responds.

"Do you mind if I make a long-distance call in the trailer?" Dustin asks.

"If that's how you want to use your lunch break. Knock yourself out," Jarret responds.

"Thanks, man," Dustin says as he pivots toward the mobile building where Jarrett typically works. The sound of hammers hitting nails, saws cutting wood for framing, and drill guns screwing in plywood and drywall begin to decline as Jarrett walks from house to house yelling at everyone to take a break. The smell of sawdust and dirt fill the air. A few of the guys jump in their trucks to go find food in town.

Dustin grabs the handrail of the metal stairwell with his left hand and swings his body around it to jog up the stairs. He enters the mobile office and nobody else is in there. This is a good time to use the phone to try to call Holly. Dustin finds the cordless phone on Jarrett's desk and pulls on the antenna to extend it. As he dials her number, he figures she won't be home and he'll leave a message. He's not sure what he'll say anyway.

After a few rings, Holly answers the phone.

"Hello?"

"Holly?" Dustin awkwardly responds.

"Dustin, is that you?" Holly says.

Dustin is a little surprised to hear an upbeat tone in her voice. The last time they talked was when Dustin decided to give Holly some space and move out for a while. Nobody was happy or upbeat during that discussion.

Maybe some time apart is already helping her, Dustin thinks.

"Hey. Yeah, it's me. I'm calling from work."

"Oh, that job worked out then?" she asks.

"Oh, yeah. There is so much work here. I can't throw a baseball without hitting a house that is being rebuilt."

Dustin finds himself loosening up a bit with the small talk.

"That's good. I mean, it's sad, but I'm glad you found a job," says Holly.

"Yeah. It's cool to see how much everyone here is supporting each other through this."

"That's good," Holly says with a positive tone. "I miss you guys," she says, abruptly changing the subject.

"We miss you too," Dustin says with some emotion swelling up. "Damon even named the dog after you."

"What? Wait. What? You guys got a dog?" Holly says in astonishment.

Dustin laughs. "Yeah. It's kind of a long story, but we basically brought home a stray." He almost doesn't believe his own story.

"That's crazy! Is Damon happy there? Does he like the dog?"

"The dog was his idea! It was hurt, and I think he just got attached to her at the vet. I thought, what the heck, at least he'll have something to do," Dustin says to simplify the story.

He's glad they're talking, but not yet ready to talk about all the deep feelings he's experiencing while on this journey. He didn't call to remind her how difficult this is for Damon either. She already knows.

"Wow," says Holly.

"Yeah. Anyway, I don't have a lot of time because I'm on my lunch break. I just thought I would call and see how you're doing, you know?"

"Well, I talked to my doctor about my anxiety, and he has some ideas. I am starting with a therapist though. I have a benefit at work to see one a few times for free," says Holly.

"Oh, that's good," Dustin says.

Holly continues, but Dustin becomes distracted as Barry, one of the other carpenters, opens the door to the trailer.

"Dude, beers at 4:30 today!" he shouts at Dustin before realizing that Dustin is on the phone. Dustin puts a thumb up to silently says thanks, and Barry apologizes by opening his eyes wide, putting his hands up, and whispering, "Sorry."

Realizing the commotion in the background, Holly stops her narrative, and says, "What was that?"

"Sorry, one of the guys needed to tell me something."

"Oh. Okay. Well, anyway, the doctor says I should think about medication. I think I should, too. I am tired of feeling overwhelmed all the time. You're taking care of Damon full time now, and I still feel overwhelmed by the dumbest things. I only realize they're small, dumb things days later though. I don't know why I can't calm down in the middle of things, you know? I don't know. Do I sound crazy?"

"No. I actually feel that way sometimes too. I think I just snap out of it more quickly than you, you know?"

Dustin is trying to relate, but he's also trying to remind her that everyone feels overwhelmed sometimes.

"Yeah," she responds and then takes a deep breath.

For Dustin, it feels good to talk about things after some separation. It feels objective, rather than trying to work things out when one of them is frustrated or feeling stressed.

"Okay, well, I'll let you get back to work then," says Holly.

"Okay. Sounds like you're feeling a little better about things though, yeah?" Dustin says, extending the conversation a little. He's looking for a sign that they're headed back toward each other. He's not yet ready to ask about their relationship directly though. The stakes feel far too high, and he doesn't want to rush her.

"Yeah. I just miss you guys," says Holly.

Dustin takes this as a positive sign, but also suddenly worries that their separation will just add to Holly's feelings of anxiety.

"Well, you can always come visit," Dustin offers.

"Okay. I'll think about it," she says.

"Okay. Good. Damon would like that," Dustin says, trying to be encouraging.

"Yeah. Me too," she says. "Okay. You better go."

"Okay. Talk to you soon," says Dustin.

"Okay, bye," says Holly.

Dustin realizes after pushing the metal antenna back into the cordless phone that he didn't tell her he loves her. He's always prided himself on telling her that he loves her every day. For some reason, now it feels like a weapon that might scare her off. He doesn't know why, but that's how it feels.

Setting the phone on Jarrett's desk, he thinks, *I guess I'll tell her next time.*

It is now close to four thirty and the crew begins packing their tools and cleaning up the site a little. As they load tool belts full of hammers, tape measures, and carpentry pencils into truck beds, they check with each other to see who is going for beers. Dustin is excited to hang out with some of the guys. They work well together, and he hasn't gotten to know many people in town outside of work.

"D, you know where the Bell Cow is?" asks Barry.

"Downtown, right?" Dustin responds.

"Yeah man. Okay, see you there," Barry says as he takes the last few steps to his truck.

Dustin has gotten to know the town relatively well by now. The Bell Cow is a bar downtown that many locals frequent. It is difficult to miss when driving by due to the giant neon cow face with a bell around its neck.

Dustin arrives at the Bell Cow and drives to the back of the building. The bar is just a few doors down from the vet clinic, and he uses the alleyway behind it to access the Bell Cow's small parking lot. It's the same alley that he used to pick up Hope from the vet. It had only been a few weeks, but it felt like a lifetime ago.

As Dustin approaches the back door to the Cow, a couple of people are outside smoking cigarettes, including one guy from the job site. Dustin quickly says hello so as not to interrupt their conversation. As he enters the bar, he walks down a dark hallway to the main part of the bar.

The twang of a steel guitar echoes down the hall, and he thinks, *Ugh, anything but country!*

He figures he'll have a good time anyway and heads past the pool tables, the jukebox, and a few tables to the actual bar. Barry is there, as is Jarrett and few other guys he recognizes from the site.

"What'll ya have?" Jarrett asks loudly.

"Beer's good," Dustin replies.

"Yeah, I know beer's good. But what do you want? A Coors, or one of them fancy new beers?" Jarrett retorts. Barry laughs and pats Dustin on the back. Jarrett's antics are clearly nothing new to the rest of the crew. Dustin realizes this is an opportunity to endear himself to the boss, and figures he better get the regular beer.

With a small smile he responds, "Coors is good, Jarrett."

"My man!" Jarrett says as he points to the bartender who overheard the entire exchange.

While beginning to make small talk with the guys, Dustin looks around the establishment.

Oh man. The country music was just the beginning.

He chuckles as he looks at bullwhips on the wall, cowboy hats on the coat rack, mounted bucks, and a coiled-up rubber rattlesnake on the bar. Underneath all the clichéd cowboy stuff is a beautiful bar made of old-growth oak and pine from the area. Beautifully stained wooden paneling covers the walls. Some of it needs to be refinished, but the wear and tear on the wood adds to the character of the place. Dustin has the feeling that if they ever renovate the place, the local patrons will riot. People who drink here want it to feel like an old-time saloon, and every nick and scratch on the walls, floor, and bar gives them just that.

Behind the bar is a stepped series of three shelves with the high-end alcohol on it. Some of the bottles have dust on them. Dustin figures this isn't the type of crowd to ask for the top-shelf drinks very often. Behind the dusty bottles are large mirrors. They make the bar feel much bigger than it actually is. A few pictures are taped to the mirror, and Dustin wonders who the people are. A couple of pictures are black and white, while others are clearly from the seventies and eighties, judging by the clothing. He wonders if they are people who frequent the place, or maybe a family that owned or worked at the bar. In any case, the rich history of this establishment is clear. Dustin appreciates this and settles into a comfort zone as he sips his beer and shakes hands with the few carpenters he hasn't yet met at the job site.

Dustin drinks his first beer relatively quickly. It feels good to drink something cold after working all day. Upon ordering the second one, he looks around the bar some more. He notices a woman by the juke-box that he hadn't noticed when he first entered the bar. She is slowly dancing to the song playing while leaning over and staring down at the jukebox. Her back is to Dustin. Two other women are standing next to her, chatting and drinking light beers. The one dancing has long, dark, curly hair. It seems familiar to Dustin, but he isn't sure why. The chorus to the song begins playing, and she turns away from the juke-box and starts singing with her two friends. They are belting out the lyrics as if they'd sung this song a hundred other times, giggling all the way. Upon seeing her face, Dustin realizes why he recognized the hair. *It's the veterinarian*, he thinks. *She's so serious every time I see her. No ponytail. No wonder I didn't notice her on the way in!*

When the chorus ends, Melissa settles back down to take a drink of her beer and looks around the bar. She instantly notices Dustin and gets a small, embarrassed smile on her face. She holds her hand up to cover her face. Dustin holds his hand up close to his shoulder, and awkwardly waves hello to Melissa. With her hand still over the bottom half of her face, and a look of surprise in her eyes, she lets out a giggle as if Dustin is the last person she expected to see in the bar. She begins walking over to him. Dustin is a generally reserved person, and he instantly becomes nervous. He moves his beer to his left hand, thinking he would say hello and shake her hand. He smiles as she draws near, and just as he begins pushing his hand toward her, she opens her arms up and offers a big hug. He awkwardly tries to pull his hand back, and it almost gets caught between their bellies. After the hug, Dustin feels more relaxed.

"What are you doing here?" Melissa says in an excited tone.

"I'm here with the guys from work," Dustin says as he waves the index finger of his beer-holding hand at the guys.

"Oh, of course," she responds with a smile.

"Shouldn't you be doctoring at your office or something?" Dustin says.

Melissa rolls her eyes and says, "I can take a day off." Then her face switches to a big smile and she says, "Today's my birthday!"

"Oh. Oh, wow. Awesome. Happy birthday!" Dustin responds.

Someone's tipsy, he thinks, chuckling quietly. *She's probably been here a while. Maybe some shots mixed in with those light beers.*

"What?" Melissa asks in a high-pitched voice.

"Nothing! I've just never seen you having this much fun!" Dustin responds. "Or any fun at all!"

"You brought me a broken stray dog!" she says.

"Yeah. I guess it was pretty serious," Dustin says as they both laugh a little more.

"You know what's fun?" Melissa says. "Dancing!"

"Oh, no way," Dustin says with a reluctant voice.

Uh oh. She's reaching for my hands.

"I'm all dirty from work! Nobody else is dancing!"

"They will," Melissa gestures toward her friends.

The song *Friends in Low Places* begins to play on the jukebox. This is one of the very few country songs that Dustin doesn't despise. With that second beer beginning to kick in, plus a large number of other patrons singing the song, Dustin finally gives in.

Ah, what the heck, he thinks as he sets his empty beer bottle on the bar.

He lets her pull his arms to guide him to an open spot near the jukebox. Dustin isn't sure how to dance to this song, so he simply sings a few of the lyrics he knows and claps along a little. Melissa's friends join them to sing along and dance. Before long, other guys in the bar are looking their way jealously but laughing and singing along anyway. Dustin finally begins moving his feet, and Melissa then takes the lead and tries to get him to dance a little more formally. She grabs his hands, swings them left and right a couple times, and then lets go of one hand to have Dustin spin her. He somehow does it all correctly and surprises himself.

Must be the beer, he thinks.

As they all laugh and sing, performing goofy dance moves to make each other laugh more, Dustin begins to think about his wife. She's the only person he's danced with in the past ten years. He's having fun, but he misses her in this moment.

At least I got to talk to her today, he thinks.

He enjoys the moment a bit more.

Wow. The doctor sure is cute when she's having fun like this, he thinks.

He looks at her face, a huge smile on it as she sings some lyrics in the direction of her friends. Dustin quickly reminds himself that she's been drinking and is just being friendly.

Why am I nervous? Just because she wants to dance and be silly on her birthday doesn't mean she's looking to get to know me or something. She knows I'm married anyway.

He quickly snaps out of his daydreaming and just enjoys the moment. The song ends and Dustin dips Melissa. She laughs and gives him another big hug.

"Can I buy you a drink for your birthday?" Dustin asks her. This gesture was as much to get off the dance floor as it was to give her a small birthday gift.

"Sure!" she responds excitedly.

They walk back over to the bar and, while waiting for two more beers, Mike from the construction crew walks up to them.

"What's going on here?" he says loudly.

Dustin is immediately worried that Mike is a jealous ex-boyfriend or something.

"This is the guy with the dog I told you about!" Melissa says to Mike.

"Oh, nice! I didn't realize it was D-man here!" Mike replies.

"D-man?" Melissa laughs to Dustin.

"Wait, how do you two know each other?" Dustin finally asks.

"She's my sister, dude!"

Sister. Of course, Dustin thinks, realizing he's let his imagination run a little too far again.

"Right on. Really is a small town, isn't it?" Dustin remarks.

The three of them talk for a while, but Dustin's mind runs to Damon. He hadn't intended to stay out late. Just a beer or two to get to know the crew. It feels good to let loose a little though. Dustin tunes out of the conversation for a second and he looks around.

I'd rather be doing this with Holly, he thinks. *I miss Damon. Time to go home*, he finally concludes.

"Okay guys. Time for me to go," he says to Melissa and Mike.

"Need to get home to Damon?" Melissa asks somewhat rhetorically.

"Yeah. Dora's been awesome, but I don't want to take advantage."

"Alright man. Glad you made it out," Mike says, extending his hand for a shake.

They shake hands and then Dustin gives Melissa a hug. It feels good to have people he can begin to call friends.

As Dustin arrives in front of Dora's house, he can see Dora on the porch. There is still daylight outside. After he closes his truck door, he waves hello to Dora and begins walking toward the porch.

"Hey, how's it going?" he says to Dora as he puts one foot on the bottom step.

"Going okay," she responds. "Boy did very well today. I think the dog may have gotten sick though."

"Really?" Dustin says. "Where are they?"

"In the back, I think," Dora responds.

"Okay, I'll go check on'em," Dustin says as he turns away from the steps.

He walks around the main house and, as he approaches his house, he can hear what sounds like crying or whimpering. He is instantly worried about both the dog and Damon. He quickens his step to the front door and throws it open. On the floor, Damon is lying next to the dog, crying.

"Damon, what's wrong buddy?" Dustin exclaims as he rushes toward Damon to pick him up.

In between sniffles, deep breaths, and crying, Damon tries to explain.

"Dad. She was fine. And then she was throwing up. I think she's sick! She ate the grass, and threw it up, and then she laid down like she's sick!"

Damon continues, but Dustin interjects, "It's okay buddy. Just take a deep breath and try to calm down."

While hugging Damon, Dustin looks at the dog. She seems fine. She doesn't usually get up to greet him. He figured it was because of how awkward her leg is with the cast. Today, she has her head up and is looking around.

She almost looks like she is concerned about Damon, he thinks.

"Okay, buddy. Why don't you show me where she barfed?"

Damon takes a deep breath and wipes away a few tears.

"Okay."

They walk outside. A few feet off the stoop, in an area where the grass is gone, there is a small pool of sputum with some blades of grass in the middle. Staring at the dirt patch with this damp pile of grass, Dustin feels relieved. Growing up, he had seen the family dogs do this a million times. He can't remember it ever amounting to anything serious.

"Did she have any other problems today?" Dustin asks Damon.

"No. We tried to play earlier, but she gets tired real fast," Damon responds, wiping his face again.

Dirt from his hands mixes with the tears and soils his shirt as he scrubs his hands against it.

"Okay. Well, that's good," Dustin says as he kneels on one knee and turns to address Damon directly. "You know what, buddy? Sometimes dogs have a small tummy ache, and they do this to try to feel better."

"Yeah, but I didn't know what to do," Damon quickly replies, becoming upset again.

"Hey. It's okay," Dustin says as he pulls Damon closer for a quick hug. He looks Damon in the face and grips his upper arms. "Next time just go tell Dora, okay? That's what she's here for, right?"

"Yeah, okay. I know," Damon says as he calms down a little. "Is she gonna be okay, Dad?"

"Yes, buddy. I think she will. Want to see if she'll drink some water?" Dustin asks.

"Okay," Damon replies tiredly.

They both turn around to find Hope looking up at them, wondering what all the fuss is about. Dustin stops thinking about the cancer. *It seems too early for that to be the problem*, he thinks.

He takes a deep breath and squats down to scratch Hope around the neck and ears. Damon joins in, seemingly feeling better. He still has a serious look on his face as he goes to get the water bowl. Damon returns, walking very carefully to avoid spilling, and Dustin is once again impressed with how well Damon is doing. Hope sniffs the bowl of water but doesn't drink.

Damon says, "Come on, Hope. You need to drink water."

His voice fades and he begins to cry again.

Dustin grabs him to hold him, and says, "What's wrong buddy?"

"I miss Mom!"

Damon bawls on Dustin's shoulder.

"I know buddy. I do too," Dustin says, failing to hold back his own tears. "It's okay to cry, you know."

"I know, Dad. I know," Damon says as he pushes his head into Dustin shoulder.

Hope sits next to them dutifully. She looks off into the trees, but knows her place is here next to Damon.

Hideaway

"How do you get it off without cutting her leg?" Dustin asks.

"Just scissors. Don't worry. I've done this plenty of times. On animals a lot bigger than Hope here, too," Melissa replies. "I mean, once I slice open the hard outer shell, it's just scissors for the rest of it."

Damon stands by and watches eagerly. It's been another three weeks, and it is time for Hope to have her cast removed. The two of them have become inseparable.

Dustin feels like he's worked more than he has at any other time in his life. It feels good. Especially now that he has some friends in the community, people who greatly appreciate the rebuild that's happening.

As Melissa clips away the gauze from Hope's leg, she says, "Now, you have to keep her close by for the next couple of weeks. I'd tell you to keep her on a leash, but I don't think there's much danger for her walking around Dora's property. Just make sure she doesn't push herself too hard before her leg is ready."

"She already tries to run sometimes, but stops because of the cast," Damon responds.

He's become much more comfortable talking to Melissa over the past few weeks. He's come out of his shell a bit in general. Dustin is happy that their temporary new home is working for them both. He figures he owes a lot to Hope and Dora in this regard. He still questions his actions in moving them here, but if Damon is any indication, they're going to be fine. Between the work and worrying about Damon and Hope, Dustin hasn't spent much time thinking about himself.

"It's okay if she runs a little, just don't let her try to herd a flock of sheep or anything," says Melissa.

This makes Damon laugh a little.

She continues, "Her leg is going to look a little funny, okay? Kinda scrawny and the hair will need to grow back. This is normal."

"Okay," Damon says.

Melissa finishes cleaning the leg after the cast is fully removed. Dustin lifts Hope off the table and onto the floor. She awkwardly tries her leg without the cast, and it is clear she's got a while before she'll feel comfortable on it again. She takes a step or two, and then shakes her healed leg a little.

"She's just not used to the air hitting her skin," Melissa says to ensure Damon isn't worried about the way she is walking. "Keep an eye on her leg, and let me know if she gets a rash, okay?"

Damon begins guiding the dog through the saloon doors and says, "Okay."

As Melissa is taking her latex gloves off, Dustin says, "You know, I never really thanked you for the dance."

He has a big smile on his face and is clearly trying to embarrass Melissa.

"Oh my god. You had to go and bring that up, didn't you?" she says, ducking her head. She is laughing along though. "I can have a few drinks on my birthday!"

"Nobody's judging!" Dustin says, laughing.

"Well. Mike told me it was a real feat to get you to dance to country music!" Melissa shoots back.

Dustin laughs.

"Did he?" Dustin responds, and then pauses for a second. "Yes. I am a big fan of ABC music," he says to Melissa with a wry smile.

"ABC music?"

"Yeah. Anything But Country music!" Dustin exclaims, as if delivering the punch line to a very funny joke.

Melissa's eyes roll, and then she laughs. "That's very funny. Hardy har har," she says flatly.

They both chuckle as they walk through the white saloon doors toward the front of the clinic. Dustin holds one of the doors for Melissa as they pass through.

For the next couple of weeks, Damon watches Hope closely to ensure her leg is okay. The fur on her recovering leg is growing back nicely, and she is more playful than ever. Dustin also keeps a close eye on the dog when he is around. To him, it seems she is aware of her ongoing recovery and is careful not to push herself too hard. Dustin again notices how intelligent the dog is during this time. She always knows where Damon is. She explores the perimeter of the property daily. It's almost as if she's looking for weak points to escape through, but Dustin doesn't think much of it because she always returns to the house. She seems to understand how good she has it with them. Damon sometimes rides his bicycle around the property, and Hope runs after him as best she can. She was recently able to outrun him for a few seconds. This is a great sign for her recovery, and Dustin trusts the dog to stay nearby even though she is no longer hobbled by the cast.

Friday, after finishing his chores, Damon decides to spend the late afternoon playing with the dog and rooting around in the old farm equipment like usual.

"Come on, Hope! Let's go for a bike ride!" he says as he climbs on his bicycle.

"Be careful with her now," Dora says, before continuing to read her book on the porch.

Dora had grown to trust both the boy and the dog in the weeks they'd been there. For a moment, she thinks about how little she's had to parent Damon while Dustin is away at work every day. She is still worried about the dog's recovery though. She insists the dog is Damon and Dustin's responsibility, but she's grown to enjoy having her around and doesn't want her to reinjure herself.

"If you go down that driveway, you better come right back," she says in a stern tone.

"We will!" he shouts back as he stands up on his bike pedals to get them moving.

He is on the grass in front of the house where pedaling the bike is always more difficult. They'd gone to the end of the driveway and back a couple of times recently. It is becoming a daily routine at this point.

As Damon begins pedaling the bike toward the gravel driveway, Hope is jumping and bouncing around him, as if to say, *Hurry up, let's get this show on the road!* This is also a routine occurrence, as Hope knows that the bike means running, and she is built for running. The herding instinct in her is too great to ignore. It compels her to move.

Soon they are off and running. Damon pulls away initially while Hope is still bouncing around on the grass. Very quickly, however, she catches up with Damon and then zooms past him. Dora sees this and thinks there is something different about Hope today. She seems more eager than usual to go for a run.

Well, she must be feeling like herself again, Dora thinks.

Damon pedals as quickly as he can to keep up with Hope. It is a game they play every day. They alternate pulling ahead of one another, but they always fell back to the same pace eventually. Today, however, Damon feels like he is pedaling as fast as ever, but not keeping up with

Hope. As they approach the end of the driveway where it meets the main road into town, Damon assumes that Hope will ease up, preparing to stop and turn around as they always do. She typically runs to the mailbox and then turns around, because they had retrieved the mail for Dora many times. It is almost like an agility course for her and she seems to love it. Hope makes it to the mailbox and takes the expected left turn around it. Damon sees this happening and is glad she is turning around because he hasn't caught up to her yet. Instead of a U-turn though, Damon's stomach sinks as he watches her make the left turn around the mailbox and then continue running along the main road.

"Hope! No! Hope, come! Hope, come!" Damon shouts trying to get the dog's attention.

He continues riding his bike, watching the dog in disbelief.

Aw man, we're gonna get in so much trouble, he thinks, panicked.

He figures he has no choice but to follow her.

At least she's not in the street, Damon thinks as he pedals as hard as he can to avoid losing her.

Hope feels so free. She can finally run with no restraints. Her leg isn't holding her back anymore. Her instinct to run to her home completely consumes her. It feels so good to act on those instincts. Even after months, her need to check on her home is as strong as ever. Even the safety and love she feels with Damon and Dustin won't hold her back this time.

Not far from Dora's property is the drive-in movie theater.

Damon sees the sign for it and thinks, *At least I still know how to get home from here. She's gotta stop running sometime soon.*

Hope takes a hard left turn down a dirt road before they reach the entry to the drive-in theater. Damon arrives at the dirt road and turns left to follow her. To his right is the fence line of the drive-in theater. He looks ahead and can see the property line for the theater coming to an end. On the other side of the drive-in theater is an old auto junkyard. The fence for the junkyard connects to the fence for the drive-in theater at the corner of each property. The junkyard looks like it is completely abandoned, or at least like nobody ever comes to this corner of it. There are many gaping holes in the fence that Damon could ride his bike through it if he wanted to. Sure enough, just as Damon sees these big holes, Hope darts right through one of them.

Arrrgghhh. I guess we're going in the junkyard, Damon thinks angrily. *I'll probably be grounded forever after this.*

Hope jukes around car parts lying on the ground and through a couple rows of dismantled rusting vehicles before slowing down. She hasn't ventured too deep into the junkyard, but Damon realizes quickly that he'll only be able to follow her on foot. He slows down just enough to dump his bike next to the fence and start running. He, too, jukes around car parts and jumps over a rusty old axle laying on the ground. Some of the cars are so stripped down and have been there so long that they are sinking into the mud. Damon thinks they look like sunken pirate ships at the bottom of the ocean, half of their carcasses buried in the sand. For a little tinkerer like Damon, the junkyard is a wonderland. He immediately drives those thoughts from his mind though, as he needs to focus on finding Hope in this mess.

Suddenly, Damon can't see her anymore.

Where the heck is she?

He feels hopeless, panicked, and upset.

This junkyard is huge. She could be anywhere!

He tries to calm down and begins walking and listening, hoping to hear some sign of her. Then he hears it: a shuffling and scratching sound. The sound isn't far away.

That's gotta be her.

He walks a little further and then sees dust floating in the air next to a car. As with many of the other cars, the body of this one is sunken into the ground a bit. It is a two-door car, and the driver's side door is missing. Some of the windows, too, are broken or missing. The car is dark blue, or at least it was at one time. The blue paint is very faded and there is a lot of rust along the edges of the car. Suddenly, Damon sees dirt fly out of the opening where the driver's side door should be. He approaches that side of the car, and figures he's finally tracked her down. He leans over to look inside the car, and there she is, panting. She looks exhausted, but happy somehow. She's laying down as Damon looks inside. As soon as she sees him, she jumps to her feet and begins scraping at the dirt again, flinging dirt and dust into the air toward Damon. His hand shields his eyes from the flying dirt.

Hope finally scrapes the metal floor pan of the car, stops digging, spins herself in a circle, and lays down again on an old, torn-up blanket. She's still panting heavily from her run.

Damon looks around the hole in the ground covered by this carcass of a car and sees food wrappers from the drive-in theater: Popcorn boxes, hot dog wrappers, and rectangular paperboard boats for nachos.

That's why she was at the drive-in! She gets food from there, Damon thinks excitedly, as if he's made a great discovery about his dog.

Damon sees a few torn and rotting blankets, some car seat covers, a few bits of clothing, some towels, and other unidentifiable bits of fabric. She'd clearly brought these things here to make herself a soft little bed. Most of it is very dirty and ruined by the weather, probably because Hope hasn't been there to clean or replenish it for some time. But Damon can imagine what a comfy little fort this would be for a dog. It's protected from the rain and wind, is probably just warm enough for a dog with her fur coat, and she has a food supply nearby at the theater. As Damon thinks of the theater, he looks up through the windshield of the car, and he can just make out the rectangular shape of one of the movie screens through the dirt and grime. He reaches out to clean off the window from the inside, but not much dirt comes off. He grabs the upper part of the doorframe on the driver's side and pulls with his arms to slide himself out of the car. He holds out the index finger on his right hand and swipes it across the windshield. He looks at his finger to see the thick layer of dirt he'd just picked up from the window. He wipes off his finger on his pants and then picks up an old, ripped towel from the ground. He uses the rag to wipe off the windshield until he can see through it to the inside of the car. Hope is still inside, still panting. Satisfied with his cleaning work on the outside of the car, Damon kneels to crawl back inside. The seats are long gone from the vehicle, so Damon piles up the remnants of a blanket and a towel to form something soft to lean against. He settles into the floor pan divot, leans against his pile of fabric, and looks out the windshield to see the complete movie screen. Next to him in the passenger side is Hope. She's now laid her head down to rest.

"You're tired, huh Hope?" Damon says as he scratches her around the neck and ears.

He lays his head down next to her, feeling a bit tired himself. The breeze along with the warmth of the sun on the outside of the car make it very cozy inside. Damon decides he should probably let Hope rest a little. A minute later, he falls asleep.

Lost

As Dustin approaches the end of Dora's gravel driveway, he sees a sheriff's cruiser parked in front of the house. He can see Dora speaking to a deputy, but he doesn't see Damon or Hope anywhere. Dustin's heart sinks, and he immediately has a sick feeling in his stomach. The deputy had turned the cruiser around in the driveway so that its taillights face the house. Dustin pulls up behind the cruiser and stops the truck abruptly. His door is open before he has shifted into park and turned off the engine. As soon as he has the keys in his hand, he exits the truck. He doesn't bother to close the door.

"Dora, what's going on?" he asks as he hurries over.

"Oh, Dustin. Damon and the dog took off about an hour ago, and they didn't come back. They were headed out to the mailbox like they always do, and I don't know why, but they didn't come back. As soon as I realized they were gone, I drove the main road, but I didn't see them. I figured I better call the sheriff."

Dora's response is very matter of fact. She doesn't seem rattled, but is clearly concerned about what might have happened to Damon on her watch.

"It's okay Dora. Kids run off sometimes," Dustin responds. He's trying to stay calm. He knows Damon, and he trusts him.

Damon would never run off without a good reason, he thinks. *He was probably chasing the dog.*

He immediately turns his attention to the officer.

"Hi, I'm Damon's dad Dustin," he says as he reaches to shake hands.

The deputy shifts his pen and notebook to his left hand.

"Hi, I'm Deputy Clark," he says as he reaches out and shakes Dustin's hand.

"So, what do we do now?" Dustin quickly asks.

"Well, judging by Dora's story, and the lack of any signs of an accident out in the road, I am fairly sure he just rode farther away than he's supposed to. Can you think of anywhere he might want to go? The candy store, or Poley's Market for a Coke or something?"

Dustin stares at the grass they're standing on.

I don't think he would do that, but it certainly seems like something I would have done when I was his age.

He finally responds to the deputy's question, "You know, I don't think so. But he's a ten-year-old boy, so who knows? My guess is the dog ran off, and he chased after it. I just hope they're not out in the forest by themselves somewhere."

"Okay. Well, the first thing is to look in town, and everywhere in between here and there. Does he have any friends? We could check with their parents?" Deputy Clark asks.

"Well. No. Not really, I guess," Dustin replies. He realizes in that moment that Damon hadn't yet made friends in town.

Kids are supposed to have friends at his age, Dustin thinks.

"Well, he hasn't gone to school here, so he hasn't met a lot of kids, you know?"

"Okay. I got his description from Dora. I'll call that in and get some other cruisers looking for him. Dora, you should stay here in case he comes home," Clark says as he waves his left hand with the pad and pen at her. He then turns to Dustin. "You want to take your truck and go looking around, that would be good. Maybe check the places he's familiar with first, you know?"

"Okay. Sounds good. What happens if we don't find him before dark?" Dustin asks.

"Well, there would be concern about them being lost in the forest, but I don't think he could go far on that bike. It's not cold enough for him to freeze or anything, but he'll be scared, ya know? We normally wait twenty-four hours to start a manhunt, but if it gets dark, we'll start looking for him on foot along the main road. We'll branch out into the forest from there. Try not to worry about that yet, though. Ninety nine percent of the time, we find these kids within two hours," the deputy concludes.

Dustin lets out a sigh. Now that he's through his initial reaction, the gravity of the situation is setting in.

"Okay. Guess we better get going then," he says.

"Okay. It's about six now. Let's check back in here in two hours," Clark says. "It'll be almost dark by then."

"Okay," Dustin and Dora respond at the same time.

Dustin drives down the main road slowly, looking down every side road and staring into the forest as much as he can while keeping the truck moving. He decides to go into town and look there as quickly as possible. Many businesses will be closed by now, but the market and a few other places are still open. The sun is now behind the trees of the forest. He convinces himself there is plenty of daylight left to find Damon, but he also knows that these thoughts are to help him remain calm in the face of a parent's worst nightmare. As he passes the drive-in movie theater, he remembers their first night in the area.

If we hadn't gone that night and brought Hope home, this probably wouldn't be happening. Funny how things go, he thinks as he scans the parking lot of the theater to make sure Damon isn't there.

Workers are just beginning to set up for theatergoers. The main gates aren't open yet. They don't open until seven o'clock. Movies usually begin at dusk, a little after eight tonight. Dustin can't imagine Damon going there this early and waiting around for a movie for that long.

No way he would do that without permission, Dustin thinks.

Dustin arrives downtown and cruises through slowly. He figures if Damon is in the market or anywhere else along the main thoroughfare, he'll see his bike.

Where the heck would the dog be though? he thinks, still in disbelief that Damon would do something this irresponsible.

As he passes the veterinary clinic, he can see some lights are still on.

This might be somewhere familiar for both Damon and the dog, he thinks. *It's worth a look anyway.*

He pulls over and gets out of the truck. The door to the clinic is locked, but he can see a shadow moving around in the back. He knocks on the door. After a few seconds, he sees Melissa's head through the saloon doorway to the back room. She squints to see who knocked, and as Dustin makes eye contact, he waves quickly back to her. Once she recognizes him, she walks to the front briskly while pulling the keys to the front door out of her pocket. She unlocks the glass door at the bottom and top, leaving the keys in the upper lock. She swings the door out toward Dustin, and he backs away to allow the door to open.

"Hey, what's going on?" Melissa asks. After looking at Dustin for a second, she realizes something is wrong. "Is Hope okay?"

"Actually, I don't know. Damon and Hope ran off today, and I am trying to find them. I thought if they were in town they might come here," he says.

"Oh no! I mean, no, I haven't seen them," she says with a look of concern. "Do you want help looking for them?"

"Oh, you don't have to do that," Dustin replies.

"Oh, knock it off. Just gimme two minutes to lock up and I'll be right out. Okay?"

"Wow. Okay. Thank you. Thanks," Dustin stammers.

Dustin again feels appreciation for having a friend in town.

Melissa heads to the back room of the clinic, lingers there for a few seconds, and then turns off the lights. She passes through the saloon doors and then stops at the counter to make a phone call.

What is she doing? Dustin thinks.

The call doesn't take long, and Melissa heads to the front. She grabs the keys from the top lock, steps outside the door with Dustin, and then locks the middle lock to the door. It is the only one she can lock from the outside. She clearly feels a sense of urgency, and Dustin appreciates this.

"I called Mike. He's going to get in his car and start looking," Melissa says as she walks past Dustin toward the truck.

"Oh. Wow. Awesome. Thank you," Dustin responds.

"Okay, let's go," Melissa says as she stands next to the truck with her hand on the door handle.

"Oh, you're going with me ..."

He bumbles a bit while pulling the keys out of his pocket and walking toward the truck. He unlocks the door, and Melissa opens it and jumps in without another word. The door squeaks as she slams it shut. Dustin jogs around the truck, opens his door, and jumps in. He again realizes they're running out of daylight, so with no more talking, he cranks the engine, throws the truck into drive, and they head out.

At the Movies

S *heesh, it's cold,* Damon thinks.

He reaches for a blanket that's not there, and rolls from his back onto his right side to curl up a bit more. As he drifts off to sleep again, he feels something wet on his face. He awkwardly wipes at it with his left hand and then tucks the hand back between his legs to keep it warm. Again, he feels something wet rubbing up against his face.

What the heck is that? he thinks as he swipes at his face some more.

After rubbing his eyes for a moment, he opens them to see Hope's big doggy face in front of him. She gives him some more licks. She enjoys the salty flavor of dried sweat on Damon's face. Damon instantly panics.

I fell asleep! And now it's dark? Oh man, my dad's gonna kill me, he thinks as he scrambles to get up.

His eyes are now adjusting to the darkness. In his peripheral vision there are bright, colorful lights flashing and moving. He remembers where he is and looks to his left through the car window. There it is. That same movie screen that was blank earlier in the daylight is now lit up in all its glory. A movie he doesn't recognize is playing. He looks over at Hope, and she is staring at the movie screen intently.

She watches the movies, Damon thinks. *She lives in here and watches the movies every night!*

Damon leans back down to get closer to Hope and enjoy the movie with her. He knows he's caused a huge problem for his dad, and for Dora. He knows he's in trouble. But he recognizes this special moment and decides to experience it.

After a few minutes, the sinking feeling of being in trouble sets back in.

"Well. We better go home, Hope," he says to the dog.

He begins moving around to get out of the car. Halfway out of the doorframe, he looks back and Hope hasn't budged an inch.

"Come on, Hope," he says as he slaps his thigh. "We gotta go home. We're in trouble."

Hope raises her head and looks at him. She looks at the movie, and then back at Damon. It is as if she's making a choice to go or stay. She's home now. It feels good. She misses the movies, the half-eaten hot dogs, the popcorn, and the smell of dust in the junkyard.

"Don't worry, Hope. We'll come back. Just wait 'til we show Dad this place," Damon says.

He scratches her around the neck for a moment, and this seems to do the trick as Hope begins to stand. She hesitates one moment more and looks at the movie screen, stretching out her body with a big yawn. Damon can see the reflection of the light and color in her eyes from the side. He realizes that this is a special place for her. He silently vows to bring her back as often as he can.

The two of them finally exit the vehicle. The light of the movie screen helps Damon navigate back to the fence where he left his bike. He climbs aboard and begins slowly riding along the dirt road that led them there. Hope trots along behind him, content in her decision to stay with Damon.

Dustin sits at the kitchen table in Dora's house. He hadn't spent much time in there since they moved in. He looks at the phone on the wall. He looks back down at the kitchen table. Like the rest of the kitchen, the table is extremely old. It is a sturdy wooden table, no doubt repaired many times. Dustin takes his elbows off the table and leans back in his chair, his right hand holding a glass of lemonade. He takes a sip. The table has dents, scratches, and knife marks in it. Like much of the stuff Dora has around, Dustin figures her attachment to this stuff is a mix of sentiment and practicality. Dustin looks again at the phone on the wall.

Should I call Holly and tell her? he thinks. *Oh god, maybe we shouldn't have moved here.*

Guilt and regret flood his mind.

What was I thinking, leaving him home all day? I knew the dog was a bad idea.

He feels a knot in his stomach as he thinks about how Holly is going to react.

Oh god, I hope Damon isn't lost in the woods.

His thoughts shift away from guilt, which suddenly feels selfish, to fear. He is scared for Damon. He sets the lemonade on the table and, as he releases his hand, he realizes it is shaking. He rubs it with his left hand and stares at the food Dora put on the table for him. He just can't eat right now. The only reason he drank the lemonade is because his mouth was dry from talking so much. The sheriff, Melissa, Dora, Mike. So many people had jumped in to help find Damon. Dustin had to explain and re-explain where to look so many times he'd become frustrated with the very people trying to help him. Dora had offered Dustin a place to sit quietly and clear his head. It is helping. The only question Dustin can't seem to answer for himself, after sitting in the kitchen for ten minutes, is whether he should call Holly.

Is it too early to tell her? It hasn't even been a full day yet, he thinks, convincing himself it is too early to panic and tell family, let alone his wife.

He thinks about Holly's anxiety. This will put it in overdrive. She'll probably have a panic attack. This has always been the conundrum Dustin faces with his wife. Good news. Bad news. He feels like she'll find something to worry about no matter how he communicates with her. Lately, he's been keeping his thoughts and feelings from her. Dealing with her reaction is frequently worse than the problem he might need her help with. It isn't all bad though, and he's not always the best partner either. The lack of sharing is what ultimately drove the wedge between them though. It isn't her fault, or his. Months of not sharing their most important feelings with each other built to a point where everything feels off balance. Which is why he's here, wondering where his boy is.

Dustin's mind wanders a bit and is then pulled back to the here and now as a tear rolls down his cheek. He begins to feel like now is a good time to come apart and just let all of his emotions out. Just as he's about to give in, his chest heaving with emotion, he sees headlights approach the house, stop, and then turn off. He squints his eyes to adjust from the lights going off, and he sees Mike's El Camino, the funny half-car, half-truck that Mike is so proud of. Dustin begins to stand, and he quickly realizes that Mike and Melissa are not alone.

As Dustin emerges from the house, holding open the squeaky screen door, he sees Mike pull a bicycle out of the bed of his El Camino. And there, standing next to Melissa by the passenger door is Damon. As Dora and a couple of deputies run over to the car, Dustin feels himself come apart inside. The only thing stopping him from dropping to his knees and sobbing is running to hold Damon. He feels his body almost float down the stairs and over to the car where Damon is.

Dustin can't feel his legs. He's never felt something like this before. It doesn't matter to him though.

Damon is okay. That's all that matters.

Dustin rushes past everyone else, grabs Damon, and picks him up to hold him. Dustin is crying as hard as he can remember ever crying before. A storm of anger, sadness, and joy all overwhelm him. He begins feeling his body again, almost as if all the blood that left him is now back. His heart is beating fast, and he feels some pressure against his left leg. He looks down, and there's Hope, sitting on the ground, but as close to Dustin as she can be. She's relieved to be home, too. Dustin wipes his tears with his left hand and, still holding Damon, kneels next to Hope. She licks his face as he scratches her around the ears. He then pushes his face against hers.

Melissa and Dora look down at the little family. Both are holding back a tear or two and smiling. One of the deputies calls in to dispatch to let them know Damon has been found and they won't need to perform a search that night. The other deputy is rolling up maps she had laid out on the hood of her cruiser. An immense sense of relief engulfs everyone on the property.

"Oh my god! Where did you guys find them?" Dustin asks.

"We were on our way here to check-in when we saw them along the road between here and the drive-in," Melissa says, a smile on her face.

Dustin stares at Melissa for a few seconds, his emotions still overwhelming him, but again thankful to have her in his life.

Dustin looks down at Damon and asks, "Are you okay, buddy?"

As he asks, he turns Damon's body left and right to get a good look at him.

Everything looks fine, he thinks.

"Yeah, Dad. We're okay," he responds, beginning to cry quietly.

"Why are you crying?" Dustin asks.

"Am I in trouble?" Damon responds.

Dustin cracks a tiny smile, thinking about the priorities of a kid. He pulls Damon against him and hugs him hard enough to crush his sternum. "No, buddy. You're not in trouble."

Going to the Movies

*I**t's late*, Dustin thinks.

He pulls the blanket over his shoulder and rolls from his back onto his right side to curl up a bit more. As he drifts off to sleep again, he feels something wet on his face. He awkwardly wipes at it with his left hand and then tucks the hand back under the blankets to keep it warm. Again, he feels something wet rubbing up against his face.

What the heck is that? he thinks as he swipes at his face some more.

After rubbing his eyes for a moment, he opens them to see Hope's big doggy face in front of him.

"Hi Hope," Dustin says as he finishes a yawn.

He gives her some scratches on the head and neck. He slept later than usual because of the previous day's events. He basically collapsed on the bed last night, exhausted from the emotional roller coaster. Now, after a full night's sleep, he begins to reflect on what happened. Nervous energy shoots through his body, but then recedes as he remembers Damon is home safe. Dustin realizes that it may be a while before he completely recovers from the fear and sadness he felt. He remembers the strange sense of relief when he didn't have to call Holly to tell her what was happening. Of course he'll tell her now, but he realizes there is still something very broken in their relationship if he is as worried about her reaction as he is about her feelings. He loves her. He has no doubts about that. The question he grapples with is whether he can shoulder her anxiety on top of all of the normal daily problems faced by a family. Her anxiety makes everything more difficult. There is something about dire situations that causes moments of clarity for a person. Dustin feels like he is seeing things more clearly this morning.

I guess this is why we're here: so I can clear my mind and figure out what to do, he thinks.

He worries about Damon being caught in the middle though.

"So, where were you guys?" Dustin asks Damon in between bites of cereal.

"Yesterday?" Damon says.

"Yes, Damon. Yesterday," Dustin says as he marvels at the obliviousness of kids sometimes. "You guys were gone all afternoon. What happened?"

Dustin sips some coffee from an old, beat-up mug.

"Well, Dad. I found Hope's home!" Damon says.

"Her home? Like, with a family and stuff?" Dustin tries to clarify.

"No Dad. She lived in the junkyard next to the drive-in."

"The drive-in theater?" Dustin asks, bewildered.

"Yeah. There's a junkyard behind it. She lives in a car and watches the movies every night," Damon responds excitedly. "Want to see it?"

"Well, hang on. What were you doing in the junkyard for that long? Didn't you know you should come home before dark?"

"We fell asleep in the car," Damon says, looking a bit embarrassed.

"Aaaah. I see. Hope stayed with you the whole time?" Dustin looks at Hope and quickly thinks about the bond they have.

"Yeah," Damon responds proudly.

"So, you came home as soon as you woke up? It was dark already?" Dustin asks.

"Yes. I didn't mean to fall asleep, Dad," Damon says, again trying to absolve himself of any wrongdoing. He takes a drink of the milk left in his bowl.

"I know, buddy. It's okay," Dustin says, rubbing Damon gently on his back. "So, should we go check out this junkyard today?"

"Yeah! I'll get my bike!" Damon yells as he slides off the edge of his bed with the almost empty cereal bowl in hand.

"Let's take my truck, buddy," Dustin says with a small smile. "Let me finish my coffee first, okay? Go brush your teeth."

"Okay!" says Damon. He rarely goes to brush his teeth with such little resistance. Dustin knows Damon is excited to show him something. He's still a bit puzzled about what to expect at the junkyard, but can't shake his curiosity.

This entire story sounds made-up. It's Saturday, though, a good day for an adventure. I just hope we don't get shot by the owner, he thinks.

Hope stands in the back of Dustin's truck, the wind blowing across her face. Her nose gently wiggles as she tries to identify all of the scents along the main road. As soon as they turn left, just before the drive-in theater, and drive down the dirt road to the junkyard, Hope begins to gallop around in the back of the truck.

Dustin sees her in the rearview mirror and comments to Damon, "She really knows where we're going, huh?"

"Yeah, Dad. I'm telling you. This is where she lived!" Damon responds.

"Okay," Dustin says, still a bit skeptical.

They reach the point in the fence line where the property to the right switches from the drive-in to the junkyard. Damon sees the giant hole in the fence where he'd left his bike to follow Hope.

"Right there, Dad!" Damon says.

Dustin looks to where Damon is pointing and sees the hole in the fence. Bit by bit, Damon's narrative of the previous day makes more and more sense.

"Stop here?" Dustin asks, almost rhetorically.

"Yeah. This is how we got in. I left my bike right here."

"Okay," Dustin says quietly, still unsure about the trespassing part of their little adventure.

He looks around, and it is clear to him that nobody ever comes to this part of the property. Trash from the drive-in blows between the cars, and the gaping holes in the fence indicate that someone long ago lost interest in maintaining the place.

Dustin shifts the truck into park, and he and Damon hop out of the cab. Dustin walks around the back of the truck to open the tailgate. Hope jumps out of the truck bed before Dustin has the tailgate completely opened. She darts through the opening in the fence, and Dustin yells after her.

"Hope!"

"It's okay, Dad. I know where she's going," Damon says with proud confidence. He walks through the fence to follow her.

Here we go, Dustin thinks as he also steps through the opening in the fence.

Dustin sees dust floating in the air, he assumes Hope kicked it up. He trusts Damon, but figures he better keep a close eye on the dog. He follows Damon past a few rows of dilapidated cars and auto parts. Looking around, he loses sight of Damon. He immediately becomes concerned and yells for him.

"Damon! Where are you?"

"I'm in here, Dad!"

Dustin looks ahead and sees more dust in the air. He walks closer and realizes that Damon has ducked down into one of the cars.

Pontiac, Dustin thinks as he looks at the emblem on the trunk lid of the car. *Gotta be from the early eighties.*

He sees scuff marks on the ground next to the driver's side door opening.

"In here, Dad!" Damon says one more time.

Dustin rests his right hand on the roof of the car, and squats down to look inside.

Wow. Damon wasn't kidding. Hope really does have a little home here, he thinks as he looks inside and sees Damon and Hope comfortably snuggled up in all of the old rags and trash.

"Wow. Look at this," Dustin says.

"I know, right? This is why Hope was in the drive-in that night. She was looking for food," Damon says.

"Yeah. That makes sense. Look at all these wrappers," Dustin says. "I bet she likes popcorn."

Dustin is smiling and sharing in Damon's daydream of Hope's life before they found her.

"You should come in here, Dad!"

"Well, buddy, I don't think I'll fit very well. Looks like it is perfect for you two though," Dustin replies.

"Yeah. We should stay until dark so you can see the best part!" Damon says.

"Best part?" Dustin questions.

"Yeah, Dad. We can watch all the movies from in here. See?" Damon says as he points through the windshield at the giant white movie screen.

"Well, how about that?" Dustin says as he rotates his body a little and rests his forearm on the upper part of the doorframe.

Looking up at the movie screen, Dustin is now fully immersed in the magic of Hope's life before they rescued her.

What an incredible dog, he thinks.

"She watches the movies every night, Dad!"

"You think so?" Dustin says. "You think she'd like to go to the drive-in with us? We haven't been in a while."

"No … we can just watch the movies from here!"

"Well … buddy … I don't think that's going to work," Dustin says.

"Come on, Dad. Why not?"

"Well first of all, I don't fit in there!" Dustin says humorously. "Really, though, we shouldn't be on this property without permission. Plus, it's not really honest to watch the movie without paying for it, is it?"

Damon is visibly disappointed, but he also knows there isn't much room to argue here.

"Come on. We'll bring the truck, and the three of us can sit in the back and watch the movie together. How about tonight? I bet she'd rather lay on a sleeping bag than in here on a bunch of trash," Dustin says.

"It's not trash, Dad! It's her house, okay?" Damon shoots back in a very protective tone.

"Oh. Sorry, bub. Okay. Well, what do you think? Is it a date?" Dustin says.

"It's not a date, Dad," Damon says in a quietly exasperated tone.

Dustin can tell Damon is easing away from his argumentative tone though.

"Oh. Okay," Dustin says. "You think she'll like it, though? She can even have a hot dog."

"Okay!" Damon says very positively.

"Cool," Dustin concludes.

Later that night, Dustin is folding a couple of blankets in his bedroom.

"Damon, will you grab the sleeping bag and put it in the back of the truck?" he yells through the doorway, unsure if Damon is in the front room or outside.

"Okay, Dad," Damon replies. "Should we take Hope's bed?"

"Yeah. Good idea. I'll get it," Dustin replies as he leaves his bedroom with the blankets and a couple of pillows.

He squeezes all of it under one arm while he leans over to pick up Hope's dog bed from the front stoop. Hope typically sleeps on Damon's bed at night. The old dog bed on the porch was there when they moved in, and there really isn't enough room inside the house to bring it in. Dustin never bothered to ask Dora about it. He wondered if it was hers or if it belonged to a previous renter. She seems to like having the dog around. *Maybe because she once had a farm dog herself?*

Dustin walks out to the truck to put the blankets and pillows in the truck bed. He pulls the handle to open the tailgate and Hope immediately knows she's going with them. She takes a big leap up onto the tailgate before Dustin has it completely down. She turns around to look at Dustin as he closes the tailgate.

"Good girl, Hope," Dustin says as he scratches her around the neck with both hands.

The sun is beginning to set, so they know it is time to get to the drive-in. Hope is pacing around the truck bed, anxious for them to depart. She is excited to go to her home again. She stares down the road away from Dora's, blinking her eyes while a light breeze blows over the hair around her neck. As the truck begins moving, the excitement takes over and she paces back and forth from driver's side to the passenger side of the truck bed. Dustin looks in the rearview mirror and sees that she is staying in the truck safely, despite the pacing. As they turn onto the main road and accelerate, Hope can smell the various scents of her home by the theater, popcorn most of all. She can also smell the exhaust and dust caused by the cars gathering in one place. She hangs her head over the driver's side of the truck bed, sniffing intently for more signs that they're going where she thinks they're going. It doesn't take long before they reach the road to the junkyard. But they pass it! Confused, Hope begins galloping around the truck bed again, barking at Dustin because he missed the turn for the dirt road they had taken this very morning. Quickly, however, they make a left turn into the drive-in theater. Hope relaxes a little as the scents of home envelop her again. She barks a few more times as Dustin pays for the truck to enter.

"Sorry about that," Dustin apologizes. "It's her first time coming out with us."

"That's okay!" the ticket attendant responds. "Just keep her in the truck while you're here."

"Will do," Dustin says as he begins driving away.

Hope is dancing around the truck bed now. She recognizes where she is, and she desperately wants to get out to scavenge for food. All this time she waited for her leg to heal. Now she's finally back to the place she thinks of as home.

Dustin backs his truck into a parking spot so that the truck bed is facing the movie screen. As he steps down out of his truck, he sees Hope in his peripheral vision. Her front paws are up on the truck bed rail, and she is ready to jump out of the truck. Dustin quickly puts his hand up and moves to stop her.

"No, Hope," he says sternly. "You need to stay in the truck here."

He grabs her collar with his right hand, places his left hand on her chest, and gently guides her back down into the truck bed. She spins in a circle, frustrated that he isn't letting her out. She barks once and moves to the other side of the truck bed.

Damon is standing there, and he puts up one finger and says, "Hope. You stay in there."

"Why don't you get in there and keep an eye on her, buddy? I'll go get us some food," Dustin says.

"Okay," Damon responds. As Dustin walks away, Damon adds, "Don't forget Hope's hot dog!"

Dustin turns around and holds up a thumb while he walks backward for a few feet.

Hope is still anxious and refuses to sit down. Damon is holding her collar to keep her in the truck while trying to also roll out the sleeping bag and set up pillows and blankets. As this is happening, the screen lights up. Instantly, Hope is mesmerized by the light coming from the screen. It flickers on and off a few times, and then begins to show some advertisements for the snack stand. Hope has seen this ad hundreds of times, and she suddenly feels calm. As she stares at the screen, Damon finishes with the blankets and pets her. This snaps her out of her trance and reminds her that Damon is there. She sniffs the air as Damon nuzzles his face into her neck.

"Come here, Hope, you can lay in your bed," Damon says as he slaps the dog bed with his hand. "I brought you an extra blanket."

Hope sees the bed and walks over to it. She steps into the bed, walks in a circle two times, and then lays down so she can see the movie screen. She takes a deep breath and sighs.

"Come on, Dad. The movie's gonna start," Damon says as Dustin approaches the truck.

"Well, you guys look comfy," Dustin says as he hands Damon a couple of sodas.

Hope raises her head to smell and realizes that Dustin has come back with some of her favorite foods.

"She's staying in her bed?" Dustin asks Damon.

"Yeah, Dad. As soon as the movie started, she laid right down," Damon says.

"Wow. Okay. What a good dog," Dustin says to Hope as he opens the tailgate.

Content to watch the movie, Hope shows no signs of trying to jump out. Dustin uses the tailgate to step up into the truck bed. As he's doing this, Damon asks him a question.

"Can we leave the tailgate down, Dad? I think she can see better with it down."

"Sure, buddy. Doesn't look like she's going anywhere," Dustin replies.

Dustin sits down on the sleeping bag next to Damon and begins unwrapping his hot dog.

"Don't forget Hope, Dad," Damon says.

"Oh yeah," Dustin says as he unwraps one of the other hot dogs and tosses it, bun and all, to Hope on her bed.

She sniffs it and wolfs it down immediately. Now she's in heaven. She realizes once again that she is safe with Dustin and Damon. She lays her head back down to watch the movie.

As the movie begins, Dustin takes a bite of his hot dog and looks up at the sky. Stars are beginning to appear, and he stares at a few of them as he chews his food. He looks back down at Damon. He's staring at the screen, happily feeding himself popcorn with one hand while clutching his soda with the other. He then looks at Hope, resting there contentedly. Dustin realizes he's given her a home. He feels good and a small smile slips across his face. Very quickly, though, he realizes one thing is missing. He looks to his right, where Holly would normally be sitting, and he feels a lump welling up in his throat. He misses her every day. Fall will be here soon, and he will have to make the decision to take Damon home for school or stay here and see how things go. The weight of the decisions, missing Holly, and being happy for the dog all hit him at once. As a tear rolls down his face, he holds the unfinished hot dog in its wrapper next to his thigh. He looks away from Damon, trying to hide his emotion, and wipes at his face with his left hand. Damon notices his dad fidgeting.

"You okay Dad?"

"Yeah, buddy. I just miss your mom," he says, trying not to break down.

"It's okay to cry, Dad," Damon says as he stares at Dustin's face.

Dustin laughs a small laugh. As he wraps his left arm around Damon to hug him, he says, "I know, buddy. I know."

Sunday Morning Call

"**T**he call went the same way a lot of our fights have gone. You know, I try to tell her how I feel, and then she treats me like I am causing some sort of problem," Dustin begins. "It's hard to describe, but it's like everything overwhelms her."

He sips his coffee from a thick-walled white ceramic mug. There's a small chip on the bottom of the mug, opposite the handle. Like a hanging fingernail that needs to be cut off, Dustin keeps touching it with his left hand while he grasps the handle with his right. He can't stop rubbing his finger on the one rough patch of this otherwise smooth mug. The diner isn't remarkably busy this morning, but plates and silverware clink in the background while Dustin stares out the window at the wet asphalt parking lot, searching for his next words. Melissa is across from him in the booth.

"What is meant as a moment of vulnerability in order to heal a wound between the two of you is perceived as an attack," Melissa says.

"Well, I'd never say it that way, but yeah. Exactly," Dustin says as he looks out the window of the diner. "I just don't think we can go back yet."

"Yet," Melissa says definitively.

"Yet," Dustin says as he realizes what a profound word that is.

"Then you haven't given up. You guys would stay here though?" Melissa asks.

"Well. I have to make a decision, because it is time to sign him up for school, you know? How's the school here, anyway?" Dustin says.

"It's good. I went there, and look how I turned out," Melissa says jokingly.

Dustin cracks a smile and laughs a little. He takes a deep breath and lifts the coffee mug to his mouth again.

"So, what else happened on the call?" Melissa asks.

Dustin sips the coffee and then swallows it.

"Well, I told her about everything that happened with the dog and Damon. She was pissed I didn't call her that night, but calmed down pretty quickly because Damon is okay, you know?" Dustin continues narrating the call for Melissa.

"I didn't want to worry you until we were sure he was missing," Dustin explains to Holly. "You couldn't do anything from there, and it had only been a couple of hours, you know?"

"I get it Dustin, but I am his mother! You should have called me!" Holly snaps.

After roughly fifteen seconds of silence, Dustin can tell Holly is calming down.

"He's okay though?" she asks.

"Yes, he's fine, Holly," Dustin says in a compassionate tone. "I promise. The whole thing ended up being not that big a deal. I mean, obviously I was scared. I was literally seconds from calling you when he showed up."

"And two strangers picked up Damon off the road?" Holly asks.

"Holly! That's ridiculous! I work with Mike. He was helping us search for Damon for half the day. And Damon knows the doctor! They're not strangers."

"Okay," Holly says curtly.

"Look. I know you're not here, Holly. But I promise, everyone we've met here is good people. You don't need to make up stories to rev yourself up."

"Don't do that Dustin," Holly says sternly.

"Do what?" Dustin says, knowing full well what he did.

"Don't turn this around and make it about me overreacting," she says.

"Well, you say outlandish stuff, Holly. How is that not overreacting?"

"I don't know these people, Dustin! You guys moved away and I don't know what's going on there!" Holly says, defending herself.

"Holly, I'm not going to do anything to put Damon in danger, okay? Please trust me that much," Dustin says, trying to calm things down.

"I know. I just miss you guys," Holly says after taking a deep breath.

"We miss you, too. We want to come home, but not until you're ready for it," Dustin says. "I need to know you're not going to end up moving out again."

"You were having a hard time too Dustin. Don't act like that was just about me. You were frustrated a lot ... really hard to be around! I'm still not sure what your problem was."

"I know," Dustin replies quietly.

"I think I'm ready," Holly replies hesitantly.

Dustin takes a deep breath. "Are you still talking to someone?"

"The therapist? Yes. I don't know if it helps. She's talking to my doctor about medication."

"Oh. Okay," Dustin says, a hint of surprise in his voice.

"What?" Holly replies.

"Oh. Nothing. I just wasn't expecting that, I guess. Is that permanent? Or just, like, for when you're having a panic attack or something?" Dustin asks.

"Dustin, I told you about it when we talked a few weeks ago."

"Oh. I guess I didn't think about it much at the time," Dustin admits, embarrassed.

"Anyway. I would take it every day. The one they're talking about is actually for anxiety and depression."

How does that work? Those two things are opposites, Dustin thinks.

"Depression? You're not depressed. Err, are you?" Dustin quickly pivots from questioning to trying to support her.

Holly sighs.

"Dustin. Depression doesn't always mean lying around in bed all day, hating life. They think I have some form of high-functioning depression. I go to work, I deal with things at home, but I don't have the motivation to do anything beyond that. You know what I'm talking about. I don't enjoy the things I should enjoy, like taking care of Damon. I love him, and …" Holly's voice begins to crack. "And I love you …" she continues, but can't get the words out.

"It's okay, Holly. We know," Dustin tries to reassure her.

He gives her a moment to collect herself. He thinks about being married to someone who must take medication every day. He remembers talking about those people when he was younger. His family used to call someone like his wife a pill popper. He never thought he would be with someone with these kinds of problems. He quickly realizes that none of that matters now.

I need to support her through this, whatever happens. She's Damon's mom, he thinks. *None of this is his fault. None of this is her fault.*

"Well. Do you want to give it a try while we're here?" Dustin asks.

Holly is silent for a while. Dustin can hear her sniffle through the phone.

She's finally able to utter, "Well, the doctor is recommending it. Maybe it is good for me to ease into it before you guys come home."

"Okay," Dustin says confidently. "You know that means he needs to start school here, right?"

"I don't know Dustin. I don't know what else to do," Holly is coming apart again.

"Hey, I didn't mean that as a bad thing. I just want to make sure we have a plan. You're not doing anything wrong."

She calms down again. "Okay," she says. "I need to go."

Dustin is frustrated by her sudden need to end this important conversation. He's trying as hard as he can to be supportive, but then he lets out a sigh and says, "Fine."

"What?" Holly says.

"Nothing. It's fine. If you gotta go, it's fine," Dustin says.

"This is really hard for me, Dustin," Holly snaps. "I don't want to cause all of these problems," her voice begins cracking. "Worrying about this shit all the time makes me tired, okay? It's exhausting."

"I know," Dustin says quietly.

Moments like this make him wonder if he can do this.

I don't want to have to do this every day for the rest of my life, he thinks. *Everything is harder than it needs to be.*

"We'll check in with you in a few days, okay?"

"Okay," Holly replies. Dustin can hear that she's still upset, but he doesn't think continuing the conversation is good for either of them.

"So, then we said bye and hung up," Dustin says to Melissa.

"You call that a fight?"

Dustin considers for a moment that their conversation wasn't a bad thing, and that he shouldn't feel like a victim from it.

"Sounds to me like you guys are focused on what is important," Melissa continues. "I've heard a lot of couples fight about stuff and, compared to what you're dealing with, it all seems pretty meaningless now that I think about it."

What I would give for a meaningless argument, Dustin thinks.

"I mean, what did you expect when you guys moved here?" Melissa asks. "That she'd fix herself and you'd go back?" Melissa curls her fingers to make air quotes.

"Well. No. I didn't think of it that way," Dustin replies, beginning to feel defensive.

"Sounds to me like this is how things had to go, you know?" Melissa concludes as she realizes she's approaching a line she shouldn't cross.

"Yeah," Dustin pauses for a moment. "I guess I didn't really have a specific plan, or whatever."

He pauses another moment.

"You need to understand though: she moved out briefly a few months ago. She was questioning the life we made for ourselves. Questioning being a mom, you know?"

"How were you doing at that time?" Melissa asks.

"What do you mean?" Dustin replies.

"Well. In my experience, people don't just leave for no reason. It takes two to tango, you know?"

"Ah. I see. Sure, I was having a hard time with everything too," Dustin says. "But don't you think moving out is a bit extreme?"

"Well, maybe the anxiety pushed her over the edge, you know? Maybe a normal person would have stayed, no matter how annoying you are."

Dustin smiles a sarcastic smile at Melissa for this comment.

"Real funny," he says.

"You know what I mean, though," Melissa continues.

"Yeah," Dustin says. "I'm sorry. I feel like this is all we ever talk about."

"Well, who else are you going to talk to?" Melissa asks, smiling.

"Yeah, but you never talk about your stuff. You must go on dates or whatever," Dustin tries to clarify.

"Ha. Yeah, well I'm taking a little break from that sort of thing while I focus on work," she replies.

"A break?"

"Umm ... yeah. I lived with someone ... for quite a while, actually. I finally had to move on. They weren't going anywhere, you know? Like ... in life" Melissa explains.

"Oh. Wow. Anyone I know?" Dustin asks.

"Well, he works with you guys. You and Mike. I don't think you know him though. His name is Reno."

"Yeah, I don't think I've worked with him yet," Dustin's eyes wander while he tries to recognize the name.

"Anyway, I don't like to talk about it. I have to say though, talking to you about your situation has helped me put some things into perspective."

"Oh ... okay," Dustin says. "But, come on, you must get asked out all the time! There's nobody in this little town you want to go out with?"

"Well, maybe," Melissa stares directly at Dustin in silence before looking out at the parking lot.

Dustin feels a strong connection to Melissa. He's made friends through work, but relationship problems aren't a typical conversation topic while framing the walls of a house. Sure, the guys know he's married and taking a break, but details beyond that don't usually come up. It's almost as if they're afraid to talk about serious things. Dustin is fine with this. Work is work, and he doesn't need to mix it with personal stuff. Having breakfast today with Melissa feels good, though. Ever since she had come with him to help find Damon, they've spent more time together. For a moment, Dustin imagines a world where he's not constantly trying to fix things. Other people's homes, a stray dog, himself, and a relationship with his wife that so often feels broken. A world where this is more than just breakfast with a friend.

Is that what I want? he thinks. *How long do I try to fix my marriage before I give up?*

"Dustin? Dustin," Melissa says as she snaps her fingers. "You're staring at me."

Dustin jerks his head. "Sorry."

They both smile politely and look away from each other.

"You're right though. I don't have anyone else to talk to." He looks at his damaged coffee cup, and then at Melissa. "Thanks."

"Anytime, okay?" she responds. "Well … I gotta take off. I promised Josephine I'd look at her horse today."

Melissa reaches for her keys lying on the table. They scrape the old Formica as she picks them up.

"Okay. I'm going to finish this," he says, holding up his coffee cup, then setting it on the table.

Dustin stands quickly to give Melissa a hug. They hug a few seconds longer than usual. Melissa figures he can use it. Dustin's not sure why he wants to hug longer, but it feels good. He says bye and sits back down to finish his coffee. Staring through the window at the parking lot again, Dustin wonders if he has enough energy left to fix his relationship.

The Fall

Summer ends and school begins. It's mid-October and leaves in the trees are beginning to yellow and fall to the ground. Dustin can't remember the change of seasons ever being so obvious or beautiful. At home, the home he still hopes to return to, roads, sidewalks, leaf blowers, and street sweepers conspire to rob people of the joy of autumn. With the number of trees around Dora's property, which somehow escaped the wrath of the fires, the colors of autumn overwhelm the senses every day. For Dustin, this is bittersweet. Experiencing the beauty means they are still not home with Holly. Dustin made the final decision to enroll Damon in a local school, and that seems to be working for them. He worries about Damon being black in a predominantly white community, but is always pleased with how accepting the children are. He knows it won't always be this way. There are hints of prejudice in this community, but nothing so obvious that Damon would notice. For now, Damon has a few friends and likes his teacher. This is enough for them to feel content in staying.

Of course, even with school starting, Damon's best friend is still Hope. Damon accepted responsibility for the dog in ways that continue to amaze and surprise Dustin. Hope is absolutely Damon's dog, and she follows him everywhere. They go to the drive-in almost every weekend. After a few weeks of this pattern, Hope now runs to the truck, anticipating their trips to the theater. Dustin doesn't understand how she knows they are going. It's as if she has an internal clock and calendar that are more accurate than any human Dustin has ever met. Or maybe she can sense the anticipation in Damon and reacts to it. Either way, she is an incredibly perceptive dog. They load Hope into the truck bed with their blankets, snacks, and supplies. Once the movie starts, she curls up next to Damon on his sleeping bag and watches the entire thing. Dustin has never seen anything like it. She stays awake, staring at the screen, until the movie ends, completely unfazed by the people and commotion around them.

Though they go to the drive-in weekly, Dustin knows that Hope and Damon are sneaking off to the junkyard occasionally. He isn't sure who is instigating the trips, but he is sure they go a few times per week. Odd knick-knacks and small car parts began appearing around the house and on Dora's property. Damon sometimes returns home with dirt all over his jeans, just as if he's been crawling around in Hope's little hovel inside that Pontiac in the junkyard. Dustin knows they found a trail through the woods that leads there. Since they're staying away from the main road and are always home before dark, he is okay with it.

One Saturday, Dustin and Damon take Hope to see Melissa at the veterinary clinic. Dustin is concerned about the dog slowing down a bit in recent weeks and figures they'd better take her in for a checkup. He's been dreading the inevitable decline of her health since the day they brought her home. With every tiny sign that something might be wrong, he feels a knot in the pit of his stomach in anticipation of what Damon will have to go through. Fortunately, most instances turned out to be false alarms or only small health problems to work through. Melissa hasn't charged them for any visits and always sends them home with free food for Hope.

"Well, how's our girl doin'?" Melissa asks after Dustin and Damon bring Hope into the back of the clinic.

With Hope on the metal table, Melissa uses a stethoscope to listen to Hope's heart.

"Well. She's been going pee-pee more often," Damon begins.

Another example of Damon taking responsibility for the dog that impressed Dustin. Dustin smiles at Melissa, proud of his son.

Melissa smirks and shifts her view from Dustin back to Damon.

"Ah. Okay Damon. We should test her for a bladder infection then. What else?"

Melissa begins studying Hope's teeth and gums. Dustin can see on her face that she doesn't like what she's seeing.

"Well, sometimes she doesn't run as far as she used to, ya know?" Damon continues.

"Yeah. Well, she is getting older," Melissa responds in a distracted tone, still staring inside Hope's mouth.

Damon finally notices Melissa's preoccupation with Hope's teeth.

"Does she have a bad tooth?" Damon asks.

"She has one or two bad ones, but they look pretty good for her age and her drive-in movie diet." Melissa smiles at Damon.

She isn't concerned about Hope's teeth, but she is concerned about the color of her gums. She only spoke about the teeth to distract Damon from her obvious concern about what she was seeing.

"Damon, can you go out front so your dad can help me take some samples for the lab?"

"What kinda samples?" Damon asks.

"Blood and urine, so we can check on that bladder infection," Melissa replies.

"How are you gonna make her go pee?" Damon asks.

"Well, all animal doctors have a magic wand. When we tap the dog with it, they pee for us."

Damon has a confused look on his face.

"It also works on little boys. So, if you don't go out front, I might have to use it on you."

Damon's eyes open wide. Now convinced Melissa is a witch, he turns abruptly like a soldier and walks through the saloon doors to the front of the clinic. Dustin and Melissa have a short laugh about it.

"Okay. What's going on?" Dustin asks.

"Well. Between the frequent urine and her discolored gums, I am worried there is some form of renal failure taking place. Not a huge surprise, actually, with the cancer she has. She had a good couple of months, but you guys might be downhill from here."

"Okay," Dustin says quietly. "Shit."

He stares at Hope for a few seconds then quietly gives her a compassionate scratch around her neck.

"Well, let me take the blood and urine samples and see if something else is going on," Melissa says in attempt to give Dustin some hope.

"Don't worry too much about sparing my feelings, okay? I knew what we were getting into when we took her," Dustin says.

"I know. We should just rule out everything else before assuming the worst though," Melissa replies.

"Yeah. Okay," Dustin says.

"Why don't you go out front with Damon? I'll use my magic wand to get that urine sample," Melissa says with a silly look.

Dustin chuckles and begins walking toward the saloon doors. Just as he approaches the doors, he turns around to ask Melissa another question.

"You know, Damon still owes you a trip to the drive-in. Do you want to go with us tonight?"

"A movie, huh?" Melissa says.

"Yeah. You know we've been going every weekend since we realized how much Hope likes it. The theater is shutting down for the winter at the end of this month. Only a couple more Saturdays left," he says in a silly tone.

"Okay," she says calmly.

"Yeah?" Dustin replies.

"Yeah. Sounds fun. Pick me up here. I'll bring a blanket."

"Yeah. It's been pretty cold lately," says Dustin.

"Okay," Melissa says.

"Okay," Dustin echoes as he realizes he's lingered in the doorway for far too long.

He turns to finish walking through the saloon doors and nearly bumps into Melissa's assistant.

"Oh. Sorry," he says to her as he finally makes his way through.

Later that day, Dustin is driving along the main street through town on their way back to the clinic. The sun is beginning to set, and Hope is in the back of the truck looking over the side of the truck bed, sniffing the air as they drive.

"I think she's mad we drove past the drive-in," Damon says.

"You think?" Dustin responds.

"She knows, Dad! She always knows when it's time to go to the movies."

"She probably thinks we're taking her to the doctor again, huh?" Dustin says.

Dustin had intended to turn down the side street to go to the back of the clinic, but as they approach the front of the building on the main street, he can see someone standing out front. A blanket is in their arms, so it becomes obvious that it is Melissa.

"Yeah. Even though she was just here this morning," Damon completes the conversation.

Dustin doesn't quite register Damon's words as he's thinking about pulling over to pick up Melissa.

As they approach, Dustin rolls down his window and, when he stops next to the curb he says, "Need a ride?"

"Oh, yuk yuk yuk," Melissa says sarcastically, poking fun at Dustin for the dorky line.

As Melissa walks around to the passenger side of the truck, Dustin says, "I thought you'd be out back."

"Yeah. I finished up with plenty of time and thought walking out front here might be easier."

Dustin doesn't have much of a reply. He smiles and shifts the truck back into drive. As he begins driving away, Melissa says hello to Damon and tells him that they don't have the test results yet. It will be a few days until they know what is wrong with Hope. Dustin has yet another moment of clarity about what lies ahead. As Melissa laughs at a terrible joke Damon just told her, Dustin tries to enjoy the moment instead of worrying about the future.

"It's kinda cold tonight," Melissa says as they all settle down in the truck bed.

"Yeah. Good thing we have these couch cushions to sit on," Damon says excitedly.

With weekend trips to the drive-in becoming such a ritual, Damon had looked for ways to make their seating arrangement more comfortable. They had taken along some cushions from an old couch on Dora's back porch a few weeks ago. This provides insulation from the cold metal truck bed as summer turns to fall and the temperature drops.

Everybody has one cushion for their back and one to go under their bottom. Sleeping bags and blankets keep them warm on top.

Hope has taken her usual spot on the passenger side of the truck bed near the open tailgate. From here, she has an unobstructed view of the movie screen. Dustin assumed Damon would settle down between he and Melissa, but Damon prefers to be near the dog. Before Dustin notices what is happening, Damon plunks himself down to the left of Dustin, on the complete opposite side of the truck bed. This leaves Melissa nowhere to sit other than between them, directly next to Dustin. Dustin decides not to make a big deal of these tight quarters and sits down in his usual spot on the driver's side of the truck bed. Melissa also realizes what has happened. She looks at Dustin and chuckles before sitting down between the two of them.

"We made it just in time, Dad. The movie's starting!" Damon says with a mouth full of popcorn.

Dustin smiles at Damon.

He doesn't seem bothered by the cold at all, he thinks.

Melissa shivers away some goose bumps as she begins warming under the blanket she brought. Dustin thinks about how he can help her warm. He considers Melissa a friend, and he thinks about the boundaries he needs to have with her. Rather than put his arm around her, he offers warmth with conversation as the advertisements play on the big screen.

"Sorry it's so cold. Was this a bad idea?"

"No way. I just need to get settled in. I'll be fine," Melissa says as she laughs quietly. "It's beautiful tonight though, right?"

"Yeah. Probably why it's so cold. Not a cloud in the sky," Dustin says. "Don't tell Damon, but sometimes I just stare at the stars while we're out here."

"I heard that, Dad," Damon interjects.

Dustin and Melissa laugh at Damon's knack for comedic timing.

"We can't see this many stars at home," Dustin continues.

"Definitely one of the advantages of living in a podunk town," Melissa says.

As Dustin stares at the sky quietly, his left hand brushes Melissa's right hand. He hadn't realized they were sitting so close. He wants to pull his hand away, but he also doesn't want to. He suddenly desperately wants to hold her hand. As if a wave of energy emanates from him, letting Melissa know what he is thinking and feeling, she suddenly turns and looks at their hands. She then lifts her head to look at Dustin. Dustin lets his hand linger close to hers for a bit longer. He can almost feel heat transferring between their hands. Melissa doesn't pull away either. Dustin lifts his hand and holds it above Melissa's. He decides he's gone too far. He finally pulls his hand away in silence.

"I'm sorry. I didn't invite you here to umm ... to," Dustin has a hard time finishing his sentence.

Melissa snaps out of the trance they both find themselves in. "Oh. No. I didn't think," she stutters through an attempt at an explanation.

"No, I'm sorry," Dustin says again. "I really miss Holly. I miss being with someone. You've been such a good friend. I'm not looking to ruin that. Or for more than that. I'm sorry. It just feels good to sit next to someone out here."

"Dustin. It's okay. I get it. I'm not ... you're a good guy, but I didn't ... I wasn't ..."

"The movie's starting!" Damon says out loud, completely oblivious to what is happening on the other side of the truck bed. Dustin and Melissa look at each other and smile away the tension. The timing of a child, perfect and terrible at the same time, has just relieved all of the pressure from the situation.

As they finally settle in quietly to watch the movie, still feeling a little embarrassed, Dustin once again realizes how much he misses Holly. His eyes well up, and a single tear makes its way from his right eye. He quickly wipes it away and collects himself. He hopes he hasn't made his friendship with Melissa awkward. He'll get through tonight, but he's already dreading his next interaction with her. Little does he know, the next time he sees her, there will be no time for pleasantries or apologies.

Gone to the Movies

"**D**ad, I really don't think she's feeling well."

Damon is lying on his bed next to Hope. He had asked Dustin to lift her up and place her there since she now has trouble jumping up on her own. Ever since the test results came back from the lab, Damon has been extra attentive to Hope. Dustin feels like Damon understands what is happening, but doesn't yet feel the full gravity of the situation. In only a few months, Hope has become Damon's best friend, playmate, and psychologist. In hindsight, Dustin wonders if any of this would have worked had they not found Hope. As he watches Damon snuggle against her, petting her and showing genuine concern, Dustin thinks about the healing power of dogs. He'd watched dogs help his wife with unbearable anxiety and depression. He sees the stability and healing that Hope provides for Damon as he makes sense of what is going on with his mom and dad. Dustin realizes in this moment what Hope has done for him, too, as he figures out what is going on in his life.

It is a Saturday in early November. Rain is pelting the wooden shingle roof of the house and streaming off the gutter-less edge of the front stoop's roof. The water pools in front of the stoop and then streams away into the forest. When Dustin joined Dora for coffee earlier, she said it was colder than she can remember it ever being in November. She also said the newspaper called for snow.

"Dora said she's going to bake all day. How about I pop in to see if she has any cookies yet?" Dustin asks Damon, trying to cheer him up.

As soon as Dustin speaks and gestures toward the door, Hope pops her head up then slides down to the floor.

"Looks like she wants to go out again."

"I just took her out, Dad," Damon grumbles.

"I know, buddy. Melissa said this might happen. Hope might think she needs to go a lot. We can't take the chance that she really needs to go. You know?" Dustin pauses for a moment to let this sink in with Damon. "I don't want to clean up pee on the floor, do you?"

"Nooo," Damon says, lazily drawing out the word as he sits up on his bed.

"What about those cookies?" Dustin asks.

"Okay," Damon answers, snapping out of his rainy-day funk.

"Cool. Keep an eye on her, okay?

"Okay."

Dustin opens the door, and Hope follows him out. He figures she won't go far in the rain, and he leaves her behind and jogs through the rain to Dora's front porch. He knows Dora will see him through the front window if she is in the kitchen. He peers through the window and can see Dora working near her stove, her back turned to him. He gives the glass a light tap, and she turns around to wave him in. Dustin was afraid he might startle her, but then he wonders if there is anything that actually could startle her.

She always seems to know more about what's happening in a situation than anyone else.

Dustin makes sure he isn't bringing too much water in with him, and then walks through the front door and turns left into the kitchen.

"Thought we might take you up on those cookies you offered earlier," he says from the doorway.

"Well, your timing is good. The batch in the oven needs less than five more minutes. You want to sit and warm up for a minute?"

"Yeah," Dustin says as he sits in the same chair where he sat and worried about Damon going missing months ago. He has another moment where he can't believe how long they've been there and how much they've experienced.

"How's Damon?" Dora asks, interrupting Dustin's deep thought.

"He's worried about the dog. You know. He's handling it well though, all things considered. I think he's more bored than anything else today with this rain."

"I bet," Dora says as she peeks in the oven. "Oh, would you look at that," she says as she turns around and looks out the front window. "Snow."

"Wow. I haven't seen that in a long time," Dustin says.

In the other house, Damon realizes Hope hasn't come back in yet and figures he better check on her.

"Hope!" he yells as he crawls off the bed and onto the padded bench under the window to look outside.

He can't see her in front of the stoop, so he thinks maybe she went with Dustin to Dora's. Suddenly he realizes it is snowing outside. With wide, excited eyes, he decides to go out to play in it. He slips his shoes on without tying the laces and heads out the door. As he steps off the front stoop, he extends his hand to feel the snow falling from the sky. He's never seen this before. He wonders what it tastes like and tilts his head back to let the snow fall into his mouth.

The snow is mostly melting as it hits the ground and Damon realizes he won't be making any snowballs yet. As he stares at the ground, he can see a few paw prints from Hope. It reminds him to look for her. He follows the prints, and realizes they are not headed toward the front of Dora's house. They track to the opening in the woods where their trail to the junkyard begins. Damon's heart skips a beat. He feels terrible that he wasn't watching her more closely. Though this wasn't the first time he had to chase her down this trail, he knows she is sick and vulnerable.

Oh, this is not good, he thinks.

He looks at the front of Dora's house and doesn't see Dustin. He makes a snap judgment to go after Hope on his own. He jets back inside the house to grab his coat. He then quickly lifts his bike from the front stoop and jumps on it. His first push slips in the mud and melting snow, but then he is off like usual, pedaling as fast as he can into the woods to go find Hope.

"Well, I hope these cookies help Damon feel better," says Dora.

"He was pretty excited when I told him it might snow today. At least that will be something for him to do. He's probably playing outside right now."

"He's never seen snow before?" Dora says in a judgmental tone.

"No," Dustin responds bashfully.

Dora has a way of saying things without actually saying them. Dustin is used to it by now, but not highly confident in his abilities as a father, he is quick to question himself. Per usual, Dora reads him like an open book.

"Well, if you're still here in December, real snow is only about thirty minutes away up in the hills," Dora says, almost as if to help Dustin feel better.

"Nice. We'll do that for sure," Dustin says as he rises from his chair. He picks up the glass plate covered with foil and says, "Thanks for the cookies, Dora."

"You're welcome," she says in her usual matter-of-fact tone.

Dustin exits Dora's house and trots down the stairs of her front porch, smiling at the snow the entire way. He heads to his left around the corner of the house, and as soon as his house is in view, he notices Damon's bike is gone.

Now why would he ride his bike in this snow and mud? Dustin thinks.

He looks around quickly, and then notices that the front door of the house is standing wide open. He is immediately angry.

It'll take an hour to heat that shack back up.

Dustin stomps toward the house, enters through the door, and immediately notices that Hope is gone, too. His mood quickly shifts from frustration to fear as he realizes that Hope is outside in this weather.

I better go find them.

Dustin checks the bedroom and bathroom quickly, sets the plate on the counter, grabs his coat, and heads outside.

As Dustin steps off the stoop, he can feel the melting snow and mud squish under his boot. After a few steps toward Dora's backyard, he's on the more stable footing of a grass lawn that hasn't completely died in the cold of late fall. He jogs to Dora's screened-in back porch. Dora sometimes feeds Hope back there, but the dog isn't there now. Standing at the top of the porch steps, he turns around and scans the entirety of the back yard and forest line. No sign of them there, or in the field to the left that used to be part of Dora's farm.

Dustin bounces down the creaking wooden steps to go back to the front of the property. Just as he passes his house, it hits him like a ton of bricks: *the junkyard!* He looks at the ground on his left, near the start of the trail to the junkyard. He immediately sees a tire track with a thin layer of melting snow on it.

Damn it! Dustin knows not to go there in this weather. Hope must have taken off.

Rather than follow the trail, Dustin decides to take the truck and drive directly to the junkyard. As the truck squeaks and rattles along the main road toward town, Dustin has a bad feeling in the pit of his stomach. He's not sure why. It's a mix of fear for Hope and worry for Damon. He's confident they won't get lost, as Damon's been down that trail many times, but he can't shake the feeling that Hope going there now is not good.

He turns left onto the dirt road next to the drive-in and, through the haze of light snowfall, he recognizes Damon's bike. It is lying down next to the spot in the fence that they crawled through last time Dustin was here. As he shifts the truck into park and opens his door, he notices the snow is turning back to rain.

Great, Dustin thinks.

He steps through the fence and, as he heads toward the Pontiac Hope used as her home, he quickens his pace.

I know they're here, why do I have this knot in the pit of my stomach?

As Dustin approaches the dark blue car, the rain increases. Mud puddles are developing all around him. He thinks he can hear noise coming from the car. He places his left hand on the top of the car and squats down to finally find Damon and Hope. Damon is facing the other way, snuggling against Hope. The sound of the rain on the metal car roof is loud enough that he hadn't heard Dustin approach.

"Damon!" Dustin says to get his attention.

Damon is visibly startled, and when he turns around to see his father, Dustin sees that he's crying. His face is covered in tears and dirt. Or maybe it is rain. Dustin isn't sure, but he knows the look on Damon's face and it's not good.

"Dad, I think she's dying!" Damon cries in agony.

Dustin's heart skips a beat. He can't believe this is happening right now, like this.

"Okay, buddy, you have to come out of there," Dustin says as his tears, too, begin welling up.

"No Dad, I can't leave her here!"

Damon is wailing now as he clutches Hope in the mud and wet muck. The rain continues to increase. It is pouring now.

"Buddy. I know you're scared, but we have to take her to the doctor. She can help us!"

"She doesn't want to go, Dad. She came here to die! She wants to die in her home!"

Dustin realizes he'll have to pull them out from under the car, but he's too big to fit in there. He tries to position himself to reach in and grab Damon, but his feet slip in the mud and he falls onto his forearm.

"Damon, please! You have to come out. I can't reach you in there. It's pouring rain! You're going to be in a giant mud puddle!"

"It doesn't matter, Dad! God! I need to stay with her!"

Dustin can't recall ever hearing Damon yell the word God before.

"She just wanted to watch more movies from here! Why'd they have to stop playing the movies! Those were keeping her alive!" Damon says as he looks at his father. "Why does she have to go away, Dad?"

Dustin quickly realizes that all of the emotions of the past few months are flooding out of Damon. He had never understood how Damon handled moving away from his mom so well. He understands now. The fear, anger, and hurt were all locked up inside of him. Hope was the only thing keeping him going. Dustin feels like everything is crashing down on him now, all at once. He slumps down next to the car in the mud and has his own small breakdown. He picks up a lug nut and throws it at the window of the car next to them.

"Fuck!" he yells as the lug nut leaves a small crack in the window. "God dammit."

Dustin is fully bawling now. After a few moments though, he remembers that Damon needs him.

"Buddy. I know it's hard to move right now. I know you're trying to protect Hope. I know she needs you. But I need you too. If you can just grab my hand, I can help you protect her. Please don't do this on your own, Damon. Let's take care of her together. Can you do that? Can you just grab my hand? I promise we'll help her," Dustin says as he extends his arm as far as he can into the car.

After a few moments to think about it, Damon is apparently able to think again. Crying, he pushes his face into Hope's neck. He suddenly turns around and grabs Dustin's hand. Dustin pulls him out of the car and hugs him harder than he can remember ever doing so before.

"It's okay, buddy. Don't worry. We'll get through this, okay?"

Damon silently nods his head, unable to speak for fear of crying uncontrollably again.

With Damon out of the way, Dustin is able to grab the corner of a bedspread that Hope is lying on. He begins pulling it to slide Hope closer to him to try to get her out. Damon suddenly kneels next to him.

"Come on, Hope. We have to go now," he says in the calmest voice he can muster.

Hope hardly reacted to Dustin trying to pull her out, but as soon as Damon speaks, she lifts her head gingerly. Her eyes are so very tired.

"Come on, Hope. It's okay. It's time to go," he continues.

Dustin can't believe the bond they have.

It's like they have their own language, he thinks, suddenly hopeful they'll be able to get her to Melissa.

Damon extends his arm into the car.

"Come on, Hope. It's okay," he says one more time.

Hope looks up at the silver screen through the windshield one more time, almost as if she's begging for one more movie to play. One last time, she'll make the choice to follow Damon and leave her home. She carefully begins to stand, and Dustin and Damon move out of the way. As soon as she is out of the car, Dustin carefully picks her up to carry her to the truck. All three of them are soaking wet and spotted with mud, but that doesn't stop Dustin from placing Hope gently into the cab of his truck.

"Let's get you guys warmed up," he says as he climbs into the truck and reaches for the heater controls. He quickly throws the truck into drive, does a three-point turn, and speeds off toward town. As they drive, Damon can see Hope fading in and out.

"Dad, I don't think she's going to be okay," he says as his voice cracks and he begins crying again.

She's dying. Right here in my truck, Dustin thinks. *Dammit!*

He speeds up and Damon clutches Hope. Her eyes are open, but she's not responding.

From behind the counter, Melissa hands the small plastic bottle of medication to a woman with her cat in a carrier, and says, "Just let me know if she has any problems eating, okay?"

Just as she completes her sentence, she sees Dustin's truck zoom up in front of the clinic, parked facing the wrong way down the street again. He parks next to the curb, just as he had the first time he brought Hope to Melissa. She realizes something is very wrong and leaves her spot behind the counter to run out front. As she exits through the front door, she sees Dustin get out of the truck, covered in mud.

"What the heck are you guys doing?"

"I think Hope's dying," Dustin says as he runs around to the passenger side of the truck to pull the dog out.

"Okay. Go ahead and bring her in," Melissa says as she runs to the front door to hold it open for them.

Dustin runs Hope through the clinic to the back and through the saloon doors. He sets Hope down on the first metal exam table he sees. Melissa and Damon enter the room. Melissa quickly puts her stethoscope in her ears, and holds it against Hope to listen.

"What happened?" she asks after a couple of seconds.

She's wondering about the dog, but also bewildered by the mud everywhere.

"She hasn't been doing well," Dustin begins.

"She's really sick, and just wanted to go to the movies one more time," says Damon, continuing to bawl.

Melissa thinks she understands now. "I'm so sorry you guys," she begins.

Before she can finish her sentence, Dustin is crying. He knows what she is going to say. He puts his hand on Hope, and it feels like the life is leaving her little body.

Melissa tries to speak again, but now she can't hold back her tears. All she can get out is, "I'm sorry you guys. She's gone." She begins crying, too.

Dustin's shoulders slump as he stands over Hope. Damon holds her and cries into her fur. Melissa places her left hand on Dustin's shoulder, trying to comfort him.

Lightning Crashes

Dustin opens the passenger side of his truck. Inside, Damon is holding Hope wrapped in a blanket that Melissa had given them at the clinic. Dustin and Damon are both still crying, but the worst fits of bawling have passed for now. Just as Dustin cradles Hope in his arms to take her to the house, Dora exits her front door and sees what is happening. She holds her hand up to her mouth in disbelief. She knew the truck had sped off earlier, but she had no idea what was happening. This is the first time Dustin has seen Dora display this much emotion. He realizes, again, how much this stray dog from the movies has touched everyone in his life. Holding back more tears, he simply nods his head at Dora and carries Hope to her bed on the front stoop. She'll stay there until they can bury her properly. Dora steps off the porch to give Damon a hug.

As Dustin stands up from Hope's bed, he can hear gravel crunching under the tires of a car coming down Dora's driveway. Curious, he wipes more tears away and walks back toward the front yard. The rain has eased, and bits of sunlight are peeking through the heavy clouds in the sky. Just behind his truck's usual resting place in the driveway Dustin sees someone with long hair step from the driver's side of the car. He continues walking toward the driveway, but has to hold up his hand to block the bright sunlight and see who it is. Finally, she comes into focus. It is Holly. His wife is here. He doesn't know why, but she has shown up at the exact moment Damon needs her. When he needs her, too.

"Holly! I can't believe you're here!" he says, his voice cracking. He quickens his steps toward her.

"Mom!" Damon yells as he runs past the truck to grab her.

He's crying, and Holly immediately has a look of concern on her face. Before she can ask what's going on, Dustin reaches her and grabs her for a hug, too. The three of them are now squeezing each other as hard as they can. Holly notices how red everyone's eyes are, including the woman standing behind her boys.

"What's going on, you guys? Why are you all crying? Why are you all muddy, Damon?"

Dustin, hardly able to get the words out, says, "The dog ... the dog just died, Holly."

Holly holds her hand up to her face in shock. "Oh my god, you guys. I'm so sorry," she says as she pulls them closer.

"What are you doing here?" Dustin asks as he finally calms down a little.

"I told you I wanted to visit! I don't know why, but I thought I would surprise you. I guess it worked," she says, wiping tears from her face.

"Yeah it did, Mom," Damon says, still pressing his face against her stomach.

"Hi, I'm Dora," Dora says from her spot where the grass meets the gravel.

"Hi. It's great to finally meet you in person," Holly says. "I wish it were under better circumstances."

"It's okay," Dora says. "In fact, why don't you all come inside? It's freezing out here."

"Oh, thank you," Holly says. "The timing of this is weird, but I have one more surprise for the boys first."

Holly lets go of Damon, walks to the rear driver's side door of her car, and opens it. She reaches in and pulls out a small dog wrapped in a blanket.

"Mom! You got a dog?" Damon exclaims as he runs over.

Tears still dripping down his face, he immediately wants to pet the dog.

As the small brown dog licks his face he asks, "What's her name?"

"He's actually a boy, and his name is Wally."

Dustin walks over to see the dog. He can't believe this is all happening in the same day.

"I know Hope can never be replaced, Damon, but I bet Wally would like to be your friend. Would you like that?"

Damon snuggles his face up against the dog and says, "Yeah."

"I don't know what your plans are, but I have a spare room in the house you can stay in," Dora says bluntly.

Holly's eyes widen and she turns and looks at Dustin. Dustin nods his head a couple of times in approval.

"That's amazing. Thank you so much, Dora."

"Let's go inside. We'll get your things later," Dora says.

As the four of them head to the main house, Holly looks at the tiny house in back and can see Hope resting on her bed inside the blanket. She slows down a little and turns to Dustin.

"I'm so sorry, Dustin."

"Thanks. It's okay. She was sick. It all happened so suddenly, though." Dustin takes a deep, fluttering breath. "I can't believe you're here. And you have a dog. I can't believe your timing."

"I really missed you," Holly says as they stop to hug again.

"I missed you, too," Dustin says after kissing her cheek and squeezing her one more time. "Let's go inside. I have a lot to tell you."